GL
NC

MARRIED LOVE AND OTHER STORIES

Tessa Hadley

WINDSOR
PARAGON

First published 2012
by Jonathan Cape
This Large Print edition published 2012
by AudioGO Ltd
by arrangement with
The Random House Group Ltd

Hardcover   ISBN: 978 1 445 85093 1
Softcover   ISBN: 978 1 445 85094 8

British Library Cataloguing in Publication Data available

Printed and bound in Great Britain by
MPG Books Group Limited

to Georgina Hammick

Contents

Contents

Married Love

Lottie announced that she was getting married.

This was at the breakfast table at her parents' house one weekend. The kitchen in that house was upstairs, its windows overlooking the garden below. It was a tall, thin, old house, comfortably untidy, worn to fit the shape of the family. The summer morning was rainy, so all the lights were on, the atmosphere close and dreamy, perfumed with toast and coffee.

—Whatever for? Lottie's mother Hattie said, and carried on reading her book. She was an English teacher, but she read crime novels at weekends: this one was about a detective in Venice.

Lottie was nineteen, but she looked more like thirteen or fourteen. She was just over five feet tall, with a tight little figure and a barrel chest; she insisted on wearing the same glasses with thick black frames that she had chosen years earlier, and her hair, the colour of washed-out straw, was pulled into pigtails.

Everyone happened to be at home that weekend, even Lottie's older brother Rufus and her sister Em, who had both moved away.

—Have you got a boyfriend at last? Em asked.

Lottie was always pale, with milky translucent skin behind a ghostly arc of freckles across her snub nose, but she seemed to be even whiter than usual that morning, blue veins standing out at her temples; she clenched her hands on either side of the place mat in front of her. They were improbable hands for a violinist: pink and plump, with short

1

blunt fingers and bitten cuticles.

—You're not taking me seriously! she cried.

A squall of rain urged against the steamed-up windowpanes, the kettle boiled, toast sprang from the toaster for no one in particular. Vaguely, they all looked at her, thinking their own thoughts. Lottie emanated intensity; her personality was like a demon trapped inside a space too small. Even as a baby she had been preternaturally perceptive and judgmental. Her talent for the violin, when it was discovered, had seemed an explanation for her surplus strength, or a solution to it; she had begun on an instrument so tiny that it looked like a Christmas-tree decoration. Now she was living with her parents while she studied for her music degree at the university.

—Why ever would you want to get married? Hattie said reasonably. —Dad and I have never felt the need.

—I'm not like you, Lottie said.

This was one of her battle cries.

—Of course, you're not like anybody, sweetheart. You're just yourself.

—For a start, I happen to have religious beliefs. I believe that marriage is a holy sacrament.

—No, you don't, Rufus said. —You've never said anything about them before.

—So when, exactly, are you getting married? Em asked sceptically. —And who to?

—How could I possibly know yet when? That's exactly what I want to talk to you about. I want to sort out a date. I want you all to be there. I want it to be a proper wedding. With a dress and everything. And bridesmaids, probably.

—So you have got a boyfriend! Em said.

2

Em was gracefully loose-jointed, with her mother's hooded, poetic eyes; she worked in the toxicology department of the city hospital.

—My husband, he's going to be.

Hattie put down her book and her coffee mug in concern. —Poppet, you're so young. There's no hurry about the marrying part. Of course, you can have a proper wedding one day if that's what you want, but there's no need to rush into anything.

Sullen white dents appeared in Lottie's cheeks where her jaw was set. —You forget that I have a whole life of my own now, as an adult, outside of this house, about which you know nothing, absolutely nothing. You don't warn Emily not to rush into anything.

—To be fair, Em said, —I'm not the one who just said I was getting married.

—Have we met him? Hattie asked. —Is he on your course?

—Is it the one with the stammer in your string quartet? asked Noah, Lottie's younger brother, who was still at school. —Tristan?

—How could you think I'd want to marry Tristan?

—Personally, I'd warn against anyone in a string quartet, Rufus said.

—Shut up, Rufus. It isn't anything to do with Tristan.

—So what's his name, then? Noah persisted.

Duncan, the children's father, arrived from his morning ritual with the *Guardian* in the bathroom upstairs. He was shorter than Hattie, stocky, densely and neatly made, with a wrinkled, ugly, interesting head; she was vague and languid, elegant, beginning to be faded. He taught special-needs kids at a local

3

comprehensive, though not the same one where Hattie taught. —What is whose name?

Alarm took flight in Hattie. —Lottie, darling, you're not pregnant, are you?

—I just don't believe this family, Lottie wailed. —There's something horrible about the way your minds work.

—Because if you're pregnant we can deal with that. It doesn't mean that you have to get married.

—Is she pregnant? Duncan asked.

—Of course I'm not.

—She says she's going to get married.

—Whatever for?

—Also that she has religious beliefs, all of a sudden.

This seemed to bother Rufus more than the marrying. He was an ironic pragmatist; he worked as a research analyst for the Cabinet Office.

—The reason, Lottie said, —is that I've met someone quite different from anyone I've ever known before, different from any of you. He's a great man. He's touched my life, and transformed it. I'm lucky he even noticed I exist.

She had a gift of vehemence, the occasional lightning flash of vision so strong that it revealed to others, for a moment, the world as it was from her perspective.

—And who is he? Em asked her, almost shyly.

—I'm not going to tell you now, Lottie said. —Not after this. Not yet.

—When you say 'great man', her father considered, —I get the feeling that you're not talking about one of your fellow students.

Hattie saw what he meant, after gaping at him for half a second. —One of your teachers! Is it?

4

Lottie, blinking behind her glasses, turned her round white face towards her mother, precarious, defiant.

—Does this teacher know that you feel this way about him?

—You seriously think I'm making it all up? I told you, he loves me. He's going to marry me.

Duncan wondered if it wasn't Edgar Lennox. — He's some kind of High Anglican, isn't he? I believe he writes religious music.

—And so? Lottie challenged. —If it was him?

—Oh, no! Hattie stood up out of her chair, uncharacteristically guttural, almost growling. — That's out of the question. Edgar Lennox. That's just not thinkable, in any way, shape or form.

—I hate it when you use that phrase, Lottie shouted, standing up, too. —Way, shape or form. It's so idiotic. It's exactly the sort of thing you would say. It just goes to show your mediocrity.

—Let's try to talk about this calmly, Duncan said.

*   *   *

Edgar Lennox was old enough to be Lottie's grandfather. Forty years older than she was, Hattie shrieked; later, it turned out to be more like forty-five. His already being married, to his second wife, was a minor difficulty compared with this. Duncan and Hattie had met him twice: once when they went to the university Open Day with Lottie, and once before that, at a private view of paintings by one of Hattie's friends. He had seemed at the time Hattie's ideal of an elderly creative artist: tall, very thin, with a shock of upstanding white hair, a face whose hollows seemed to have been carved

5

out by suffering, tanned skin as soft as leather, a charcoal-grey linen shirt.

—When you say he's touched your life, could we be quite specific about this? Duncan said. —Has he actually, in the ordinary, non-transcendent sense of the word, touched you?

Em protested in disgust. —Dad, you can't ask her that!

Em had been crying; her eyelids were swollen and puffy, and her face was blotched. Hattie's and Lottie's eyes were hot and dry.

Hattie turned on him. —How can you put it like that? How could you make it into one of your clever remarks?

—If you're asking, Lottie said, —whether we've consummated our relationship, then, yes, of course we have. What do you think we are? We're lovers.

—Naturally, I'm making a formal complaint to the university, Hattie said. —He'll lose his job. There's no question about that.

—That'll be sensible, won't it? Em said. —Then if they are married he won't be able to support her.

—You're sure she isn't making all this up? Rufus suggested.

—Think what you like, Lottie said. —You'll soon know.

She sat with her mouth primly shut, shining with a tragic light. Beyond the kitchen windows, veils of rain drove sideways into the sodden skirts of the horse chestnut tree, darkening the pink flowers. Hattie said that the whole thing reminded her of when she was at art college, and a friend of hers had heard suddenly that her sister was on the point of entering a convent, a closed order that allowed no contact with family or friends.

—We all piled on to a train and went up to Leeds together on the spur of the moment, six or seven of us who were close then, and met this sister in a tea shop, and tried to convince her of everything in the world that was worth staying for.

—Don't be ridiculous, Mum. I'm not going into a convent.

—Did it work? Noah asked. —Did you convince her?

Hattie frowned and pressed her knuckles to her forehead. —I can't remember whether she went into the convent or not in the end. Perhaps she did. I can only remember the tea shop, and after that a pub, and trying to think of all the things we couldn't bear to leave behind, and getting gradually drunker and drunker.

—This isn't the same thing, Duncan said firmly. — And we aren't at anything like that stage yet, anyway.

Lottie stared at them in genuine bewilderment. —I don't understand you all, she said. —How can you not want for me what I want?

*   *   *

Noah saw his parents leave the house late in the evening. His bedroom was in the attic, he was sitting on the sill of his little casement window, his feet in the lead-lined gutter that ran like a trough the length of the Georgian terrace, looking down over the stone parapet into the street, four storeys below. Though it was strictly forbidden, he had liked to sit this way ever since he was given this bedroom when he was eight; he used to fit into the small space perfectly, but now he had to squeeze, and his knees were jackknifed up in front of his face. Rain was sluicing down the slate

7

roof into the gutter. In the light of the street lamps, the road shone black; parked cars were plastered with wet leaves from the beeches and horse chestnuts in the muddy triangle of public garden opposite. His mother's high heels scraped fiercely in the empty street as she crossed to the car: she must have dressed up in her teaching clothes for the occasion. She was hanging on tightly to the strap of the bag slung over her shoulder. She and Duncan dithered around the car under the half-globes of their umbrellas, probably quarrelling about who should drive; they seemed as small as dolls from where he watched. He supposed they were going to try to find Edgar Lennox at his house; they had been calling him on the phone all day, without getting through. It was strange to think of the two households, more or less unknown to each other before tonight, connected by this drama, awake in the city when everyone else was getting ready for sleep.

Hours later—he wasn't sure how many hours, as he'd fallen asleep at his desk while revising for the geography GCSE exam he had on Monday morning—Noah woke to the sound of his mother's voice in the house again. She sounded like she did when she'd had too much wine at parties: rash and loud, extravagantly righteous. He went out to listen, leaning over the banister and sliding noiselessly down, a few steps at a time. The steep and narrow staircase, the core of the skinny house, drew sound upward. Above his head, an ancient skylight as wide as the stairwell rattled under the rain, leaking into a strategically placed bucket. His parents and Rufus and Em were crowded at the foot of the stairs, in the hallway's jumble of boots and bikes and baskets, junk mail, umbrellas dripping on the grey and white tiles.

His mother still had her fawn mac on.

—I thought he'd be ashamed, she was saying, —if I told him that Lottie was marrying him because she thinks he's a great man. But it was obvious that he thinks he is one, too.

—Is he one? Rufus asked.

—Don't be ridiculous. What would he be doing teaching in a second-rate music department at a provincial university?

—I thought you said the department was something wonderful.

—That was before this.

—He does some film and television work if he can get it, Duncan said. —All fairly high-toned. And he writes for the cathedral choir. Anyway, greatness wouldn't necessarily make him any better, as far as Lottie's concerned.

—He said that he could see how it must look from our point of view, from what he called 'any ordinary perspective'.

—How dare he think we're ordinary? Em raged.

—He said that the erotic drive was a creative force he felt he had to submit to.

—Oh, yuck! Hideous!

—Hattie, he didn't say that, exactly.

—And what was his wife like? Was she there? What's her name?

—Valerie. Val, he calls her. She was frosty. She said, 'Whatever happens, I keep this house', as if that were something we were after. The house wasn't what you'd expect, anyway, not arty: stuffy and old-fashioned. I should think the wife's about my age, but she's let herself go—grey ponytail, no make-up, one of those dowdy skirts with an elastic waistband.

—She was fierce, Duncan said. —I'd have been

9

frightened of her, in his shoes.

—She wouldn't sit down; she stood up with her back against the wall, as if she were mounting guard over something. All she said was that Lottie would soon learn. They have a son, about the same age as Noah.

—Did she know about it all already?

—She hadn't known for long—he'd just told her. She'd been crying.

—We walked in on it all. We were the aftershock.

—Where is Lottie, anyway?

—It has to run its course, Duncan said. —We're not in a position to prevent anything.

—It can't be allowed to run its course, Duncan! What if they actually went through with this crazy wedding?

He groaned consolingly. —She's an adult—she's nineteen. Worse things happen at sea.

Noah turned and saw that Lottie was standing in her nightdress on the stairs just behind him. She put her finger to her lips; her eyes behind her glasses were black pits. She was shaken with waves of violent trembling, gripping the banister to steady herself, probably because she had swallowed too many of the caffeine tablets she claimed she was addicted to; and no doubt also because she was exalted and frightened at her ability to raise this storm in adult lives. Noah felt a familiar irritation with her exaggerations, mixed with protectiveness. He and Lottie had grown up very close, adrift from the rest of the family in their bedrooms in the attic. He knew how passionately she succumbed to the roles she dreamed up for herself. She won't be able to get out of this one, he thought. She can't stop now.

*　　　*　　　*

The wedding was held in a registry office, with a blessing at a church afterwards; Edgar insisted on the Elizabethan Prayer Book and the Authorized Version of the Bible. He composed, for the occasion, a setting for Spenser's *Epithalamion* and one of his students sang it at the reception, which was in a sixteenth-century manor house with a famous garden that belonged to the university. Hattie refused to have anything to do with it all; she shut herself in at home with her detective novels. Noah drank a lot and befriended Edgar's son, Harold, who had floppy pale hair and a choral scholarship at a cathedral school; he jumped like a shot bird if anyone spoke to him unexpectedly.

Emily said that Lottie's white suit looked like a child's nurse outfit—all it needed was a sewn-on red cross. Lottie was wearing contact lenses, and without her glasses her face seemed weakly, blandly expectant. A white flower fastened behind her ear slid gradually down her cheek during the course of the afternoon until it was bobbing against her chin. She clung to Edgar with uncharacteristic little movements, touching at his hand with her fingertips, dropping her forehead to rest against his upper arm while he spoke, or throwing back her head to gaze into his face.

—It won't last, Duncan reassured his other children.

To Edgar's credit, he seemed sheepish under the family's scrutiny, and did his best to jolly Lottie along, circulating with her arm tucked into his, playing the gentle public man, distinguished in his extreme thinness, his suit made out of some kind

11

of rough grey silk. You would have picked him out in any gathering as subtle and thoughtful and well informed. But there weren't really quite enough people at the reception to make it feel like a success: the atmosphere was constrained; the sun never came out from behind a mottled thick lid of cloud. After the drink ran out and the students had melted away, too much dispiriting white hair seemed to show up in the knots of guests remaining, like snow in the flower beds. Duncan overheard someone, sotto voce, refer to the newly-weds as 'Little Nell and her grandfather'.

Valerie phoned Lottie a week or so after the wedding to ask whether she knew that Edgar had tried the same thing the year before with the student who had sung at the reception, a tall beautiful black girl with a career ahead of her: she'd had the sense to tell him where to go. —To fuck off, Valerie enjoyed enunciating precisely, as if she hadn't often used that word. Everyone knew about this because Valerie had also telephoned Hattie. When Hattie asked Lottie about it, Lottie only made one of her horrible new gestures, folding her hands together and letting her head droop, smiling secretively into her lap. —It's all right, Mum, she said. —He tells me everything. We don't have secrets. Soraya is an exceptional, gifted young woman. I love her, too.

Hattie hated the way every opinion Lottie offered now seemed to come from both of them: we like this, we always do that, we don't like this. They didn't like supermarkets; they didn't like muzak in restaurants; they didn't like television costume dramas. As Duncan put it, they generally found that the modern world came out disappointingly below their expectations. Hattie said that she wasn't ready to have Edgar in her house yet.

The university agreed that it was acceptable for Lottie to continue with her studies, as long as she didn't take any of Edgar's classes; but of course he carried on working with her on her violin playing. Her old energy seemed to be directed inward now; she glowed with the promise of her future. She grew paler than ever, and wore her hair loose, and bought silky indeterminate dresses at charity shops. Hattie saw her unexpectedly from behind once and thought for a moment that her own daughter was a stranger, a stumpy little child playing on the streets in clothes from a dressing-up box. Edgar and Lottie were renting a flat not far from Hattie and Duncan: tiny, with an awful galley kitchen and the landlord's furniture, but filled with music. Edgar had to pay about half his salary to Valerie to cover his share of the mortgage on the house and the part of Harold's schooling that wasn't paid for by the scholarship, so he and Lottie were pretty hard up, but at first they carried this off, too, as if it were a sign of something rare and fine.

—God knows what they eat, Hattie said. —Lottie doesn't know how to boil an egg. Probably Edgar doesn't know how to boil one, either. I'll bet he's had women running round him all his life.

Noah reported that they often had Chinese takeaway.

*   *   *

Then Lottie began to have babies. Familiarity had just started to silt up around the whole improbable idea of her and Edgar as a couple—high-minded, humourless, poignant in their unworldliness— when everything jolted on to this new track. Three

13

diminutive girls arrived in quick succession, and life at Lottie and Edgar's, which had seemed to drift with eighteenth-century underwater slowness, snapped into noisy, earthy and chaotic contemporaneity. Lottie in pregnancy was as swollen as a beach ball; afterwards she never recovered her neat boxy little figure, or that dreamily submissive phase of her personality. She became bossy, busy, cross; she abandoned her degree. She chopped off her hair with her own scissors, and mostly wore baggy tracksuit bottoms and T-shirts. Their tiny flat was submerged under packs of disposable nappies, cots, toys, washing, nursing bras and breast pads, a playpen, books on babies, books for babies. The tenant below them left in disgust, and they moved downstairs for the sake of the extra bedroom. As soon as the girls could toddle, they trashed Edgar's expensive audio equipment. He had to spend more and more time in his room at the university, anyway—he couldn't afford to turn down any commissions. Now Lottie spoke with emotion only about her children and about money.

The girls were all christened, but Lottie was more managerial than rapt during the ceremonies: Had everyone turned up who had promised? (Rufus wouldn't.) Was Noah capturing the important moments on his video camera? Why was Harold in a mood? With the fervour of a convert to practicality, she planned her days and steered through them. Duncan taught her to drive and she bought a battered old Ford Granada, unsubtle as a tank, and fitted it with child seats, ferrying the girls around from nursery to swimming to birthday parties to baby gym. She was impatient if anyone tried to turn the conversation around to art or music, unless it was Tiny Tots ballet. She seemed to be carrying around,

14

under the surface of her intolerant contempt for idleness, a burning unexpressed message about her used-up youth, her put-aside talent.

—She ought to be abashed, Hattie said once. — We warned her. Instead, she seems to be angry with us.

Hattie had been longing for early retirement but she decided against it, fearing that the empty days might only fill up with grandchildren. She believed that in the mirror she could see the signs in her face—like threads drawn tight—of the strain of those extra years of teaching she had not wanted.

—Poor old Lottie, Duncan said.

—Lottie isn't old. Poor Edgar.

At weekends, Duncan sometimes came home to find Edgar taking refuge at his kitchen table, drinking tea while the children made scones or collages with Hattie. Edgar didn't do badly with them, considering, but it could take him three-quarters of an hour to get all three little girls stuffed into coats and mittens and boots and pushchairs, ready to go. Physically, he was rather meticulous and pedantic. If Lottie was with him, she would push his fine long fingers brusquely aside and take over the zipping and buttoning. — Here, let me do it, she'd snap. To his credit, Edgar didn't seem to resent the intrusion of the babies into his life, or even to be wiped out by them, exactly: he gave himself over to their existence with a kind of bemused wonder. He drew himself down to their level, noticing everything they noticed, becoming involved in their childish chatter and speculation as Lottie didn't have time to be. They adored him— they ran to cling to his legs whenever their mummy was cross. Edgar's appearance was diminished, though, from what it had once been: his white hair

15

had thinned and was cut shorter and lay down more tamely on his head; his clothes were the ordinary dull things anyone could buy in a supermarket. Hattie realised with surprise that it must have been Valerie who was behind the charcoal-grey linen shirts, the silk suits, the whole production of Edgar as exceptional and distinguished.

When Emily got pregnant with her first child, Lottie's youngest was nine months old and Charis, her eldest, was five. Lottie dumped black bags of used baby things on Emily one evening without warning. —Chuck them out if you don't want them, she said. —I've got no more use for them. I've had my tubes tied.

*   *   *

After he finished his degree, Noah went to London and found work intermittently as an assistant cameraman on small film projects. He dropped in at Lottie's whenever he came home, and they fell easily into their old companionable closeness. She fed him whatever awful mush she had cooked for tea. He was useful for swinging his nieces about and throwing them in the air, all the rough play that Edgar had to be careful of. Often, Edgar wasn't there; Noah assumed that he was working in his room at the university.

One summer evening, Noah was lying on his back on the floor in Lottie's front room. Two floor-length sash windows opened from this room on to a wrought-iron balcony; Lottie had made Edgar fix bars across, to stop the girls from getting out there. A warm incense of balsam poplar mingled with petrol fumes breathed from the street. They had drunk the bottle of wine that Noah had brought with

16

their teatime mush; while they were giving the girls a bath, Lottie had produced triumphantly from the back of a cupboard a sticky bottle half full of Bacardi that nobody liked, and now they were drinking that, mixed with blackcurrant cordial because that was all she had. —We'll be horribly, pinkly, sick, Lottie predicted. The girls were asleep at last. While Noah lay supine, Lottie crawled round him on her hands and knees, grunting with the effort, putting away in primary-coloured plastic boxes the primary-coloured toys that were strewn like strange manna all around the carpet.

—I'm grey, she complained. —My life's so grey.

—When does Edgar get back from work?

—Don't be thick, Noah. Ed's retired. The university couldn't keep on employing him for ever. He's seventy-two this year. Why d'you think I've been going on to you about how hard-up we are?

—Where is he, then?

—At Valerie's, I expect.

Noah opened his eyes in surprise, angling his head up from the floor to get a look at her. —Oh!

—That's where he usually is.

—Is that all right?

—Why shouldn't he? When we've been paying half the mortgage for all these years—at least that's finished at last, thank Christ. There's a room there where he can work; it's impossible here. And we don't have space for a piano. He still likes to write at a piano, before he puts it on the computer.

—So they get on OK, him and Valerie?

—She brings him coffee and plates of sandwiches while he's working. She unplugs the phone in the hall, in case it disturbs him. He plays things to her. I expect that sometimes while he's in the throes of composition he forgets he doesn't live there any more, in that quiet house.

—Mum said the house was old-fashioned.

—It is old-fashioned. Full of antiques, from Valerie's mother, but Valerie wouldn't know how to show them off. Valerie doesn't have a showing-off bone in her body. She's all complications. She's a gifted cellist, apparently, but she can't play in public.

—I suppose you've got to know her.

Lottie aimed bricks at a box. —Not in the face-to-face sense. Occasionally she and I do have to talk, about Harold's allowance or whatever.

—He doesn't still have an allowance?

—Not after we had the talk. On my wedding night, I tell you, it was like Bartók's *Bluebeard's Castle*. My metaphorical wedding night—I don't actually mean that one night in particular. Behind the first door, the torture chamber; behind the second door, a lake of tears, and so on. Behind the last door were his other wives, alive and well. Well, the first one isn't exactly alive, but I could tell you all about her.

—I'd forgotten there was a first one.

—Danish, actress, had problems with her abusive father, drank.

—He goes on about them?

—Not really. They're just his life—they crop up, as you can imagine. There's a lot of life behind him to crop up. Don't forget, once Valerie was the one he ran away with.

—I'd never thought of it like that.

—Were the babies my revenge? Poor Ed, I've nearly killed him.

Lottie lay down on the floor, head to toe with Noah, holding her glass on the soft mound of her stomach, tilting the viscous red drink backward and

18

forward as she breathed.

—Do you know what I did the other week? I was so angry about something—can't remember what—that I drove up to the recycling depot with the babies in the back of the car to throw my violin into the skip for miscellaneous household waste.

Noah sat upright. —The one Mum and Dad bought for you? Didn't that cost loads of money? Thousands?

—I didn't actually do it. I looked down into the skip and got the violin out of the case to throw, and then I put it away again. Apart from anything else, I told myself, I could always sell it. And it's possible I might want to start again, when this is over. But probably I won't, ever.

—Is Edgar any good? Noah demanded drunkenly, suddenly aggressive. —I mean, is his music really, actually any good?

—Noah, how can you ask that? You're not allowed to ask that.

Although Lottie protested, the question seemed intimately known to her, as if she had thrown herself too often against its closed door. —How can I judge? I can't tell. I think he's good. He's writing something at the moment, for strings. It'll get a premiere at the Festival. It's something new, different. Actually, I think it might be lovely.

Just then they heard Edgar's deliberate slow step on the stairs, his key in the door to the flat.

—He pretends this new piece is for me. But I know it's not about me.

Edgar stood squinting at them from the doorway, getting used to the light; his khaki hooded waterproof and stooped shoulders gave him, incongruously, the toughened, bemused aura of an explorer returned.

19

Noah imagined how infantile he and Lottie must look, lying on the floor among the toys with their bright red drinks, and how uninteresting youth must sometimes seem.

—We're finishing up that Bacardi, Ed, Lottie said, enunciating too carefully. —Do you want some?

Edgar's eyes these days had retreated behind his jutting cheekbones and sprouting eyebrows; something suave had gone out of his manner. He said that he would rather have a hot drink. Forgetfully he waited, as if he expected Lottie to jump up and make it for him. When he remembered after a moment, and went into the kitchen to do it himself, he didn't imply the least reproach; he was merely absorbed, as if his thoughts were elsewhere. Noah saw how hungrily from where she lay Lottie followed the ordinary kitchen music—the crescendo of the kettle, the chatter of crockery, the punctuation of cupboard doors, the chiming of the spoon in the cup—as if she might hear in it something that was meant for her.

Friendly Fire

Shelley was helping out her friend Pam. Pam had her own cleaning business, but her employees were so unreliable that she ended up doing half the work herself. She'd been hired to do a scrub-off— meaning a thorough cleaning, right down to basics—at an industrial warehouse somewhere at the edge of the city. Shelley had agreed to go along; it was a few weeks before Christmas, and she could do with the extra money. When she went outside to wait for Pam it was still night, the stars showing in the sky like flecks of broken glass. Pam was late as usual, but Shelley hadn't wanted to wait inside in case the doorbell woke the others: her daughter and baby granddaughter were asleep upstairs. She felt herself growing heavy and thick with cold. You forgot about the cold—the house had central heating, and winters weren't like they used to be. When Shelley was a child, she'd wrapped her scarf around her head and mouth on the way to school, trying to trap the warmth of her breath inside; these days, you hardly needed a scarf. The phase of life Shelley was in now, anyway, the heat of her body came and went in blasts, and she had a horror of being caught out in tight clothes.

She could have stamped her feet or flung her arms around, but it was too early in the morning; instead, she let the cold creep into her as if she were made of stone. When the car pulled up at last, she could barely even move towards it, though she could see Pam lit up inside, peering out through the window, looking for her. Pam always drove

21

with the interior light on. She treated her car like just another room in her house—while she was driving, she'd fiddle around with piles of paper and bits of crocheted blanket and boxes of tissues on the passenger seat, hanging on to the steering wheel with her other hand. She was a danger on the road, but Shelley didn't drive. For a moment, before she headed over to the car, Shelley imagined herself as Pam was seeing her—just another pillar of dark, like the hedge and the phone box and the pebble-dashed end wall of the kitchen extension. She and her husband Roy lived on what had been a council estate, although they had been buying their house for years now.

Pam was fat like a limp saggy cushion, very short, with permed yellow curls that were growing out grey; her face was crumpled like an ancient baby's. Roy said that Pam and Shelley side by side looked like Little and Large, because Shelley was tall and thin. She had never been one to eat too much. Her only weakness was tea with sugar; she drank a lot of that—couldn't give it up. Her daughter Kerry said her insides must be black.

—Hiya, Shell.

Pam leaned over to open the door, then began throwing stuff into the back seat. —I've had a letter off the hospital about my gallstones.

All Pam's conversations began as if you hadn't stopped talking since you last saw her; they were as cluttered as her car. The heater was on high, belting out a stinging warmth that smelled of the little cardboard pine-tree air freshener dangling from the rearview mirror.

—What gallstones?

—Well, they may not be. I've got to go in on the

22

fifteenth. Typical—that's the day John wants the car to go and see his sister in Tamworth. I said to him, 'You'll have to fix another day.' He says he doesn't want to mess her around. Don't get me wrong—I've got a lot of time for his sister.

Pam's husband John was meant to do the books for the cleaning business, but as far as Shelley could see he sat in front of the telly and did nothing, while Pam went driving about all over the place like a mad thing—and the car was forever breaking down. John used to be a plasterer. He was supposed to have damaged his leg years ago, falling from a scaffold, but Shelley had seen him limp with a different leg on different days. Pam was a good worker, though. Once she got into a job, she stuck at it until the sweat was running off her, she wouldn't give up. Shelley was like that too. They didn't make a bad team.

They crossed the river. It was at low tide, sunk to a twisting channel between flanks of mud glinting with moonlight. A notice outside the red brick warehouse, which was not much more than a two-storey shed, warned that it was patrolled by security dogs, but there was no sign of them. Pam stopped in the empty car park, and they got out some of their kit from the boot; the employers were supposed to provide equipment, but sometimes they left out broken old mops or brooms so heavy you could hardly lift them.

*　　　*　　　*

Shelley switched her mobile off before she started working; otherwise, she couldn't concentrate. Her son Anthony was in Afghanistan. Roy said that statistically Anthony would be in more danger if he

23

were still playing with his rugby club, but Shelley was always waiting for some dreadful kind of message. There was a big operation under way. Anthony had told them that he'd had his leave cancelled, but Roy was sure he'd volunteered to stay. It wasn't only that her son might be killed or injured—Shelley pushed those possibilities right down in her mind until they weren't any more than shapes in the dark. She never watched the news; she only listened in from the kitchen while the others watched it. But when there was that fuss about the friendly-fire incident with the Danish soldiers, she fixated on the idea that Anthony had been involved in it, even though Roy insisted that he'd been nowhere near where it had happened. —Why d'you have to make up trouble, he said, —as if there wasn't enough of the real thing?

Inside, the warehouse was a big open hall, divided into metal cages piled high with different grades of insulating material. Yellow forklifts were parked as if resting in the aisles between them. Fibrous orange dust was everywhere, but Shelley and Pam weren't contracted to clean the warehouse itself—the men were supposed to do that. The canteen and toilets were along one wall, the offices upstairs on a sort of mezzanine. You could see why they needed the scrub-off: the regular cleaners hadn't been doing much of a job. All the pipes in the canteen were thick with dust. Under the plate rack on the draining board and at the bottom of the plastic pot for the cutlery was a murky grey sludge. The toilets stank; the cleaners had actually mopped around a roll of toilet paper that had fallen on to the floor, not bothering to pick it up. One of the sinks was blocked and full of scummy water.

To be fair, Pam said, the boss had only been paying the regulars for two hours a day, which wasn't enough: there was a kitchenette and a separate toilet upstairs with the offices, too. Two hours would be just enough time to wash the cups and plates and put them away, and give the toilets a quick once-over; to do the place properly you'd need four hours at least. Shelley knew what it was like if you had a job like this: you got your regular routine going, and then that was all you saw; you played your music and went into a kind of dream, wiping and sweeping, until you hardly knew what you were doing, just going through the motions. But she wasn't the sort of person who took on this kind of work as a regular thing. She had a proper job at a school as a lunchtime supervisor. She wasn't such a fool, either—she knew that somewhere like this, if they saw that you were keeping it clean in two hours they'd cut you down to an hour and a half. Why should you care whether the place was as filthy as hell?

*　　　*　　　*

By the time the men came in at eight, Shelley and Pam had finished the kitchen and Shelley had just got going on the toilets. One man barged in, despite the notice she'd put on the door, and then looked surprised to see her scrubbing on her knees with her backside in the air.

—What d'you need to go for already? she said, pulling out one earphone from her music player. — You only just got here!

He was sheepish. —Two cups of tea for

25

breakfast. Bladder control's not what it used to be.

—Use the one upstairs.

—Don't tell me they piss the same stuff as we do?

—You're not coming near my toilets until they're spotless.

It was better when the men were in, there was always the opportunity for a bit of a joke. He probably liked the sight of my backside better than my face, she thought when she got up to refill her bucket and caught her reflection in the mirror above one of the sinks, a square of polished tin screwed on to the wall. Once upon a time, the idea of the man enjoying looking at her would have started something, one of those games, looking out for him among the others, bantering with him. She used to make herself dizzy, imagining other men, though it hadn't gone further in reality, or not very often. She could remember once, not all that long ago, when she would have fallen to the bedroom floor if Roy hadn't held her up while they were kissing—she'd been dragged down so powerfully by her own sensations. If it wasn't the thought of Roy that had started her off that night, he hadn't known it—he'd got lucky anyway. In the last year or so, those dizzy fantasies and their sensations had stopped, cut off as abruptly as if someone had pulled a switch, only the memory of them left like markers on the surface above deep water. She supposed that it was her time of life, though it felt more as if she were holding herself apart from her own body, afraid to leave off being vigilant for a moment.

There were worse things than going to fat like Pam, Shelley thought. In the mirror she looked

26

sharp enough to cut something, hard fixed lines beside her mouth, her eyes too big, her cheekbones jutting like knuckles under her skin, up to her elbows in dirty work, cleaning toilets. The wall behind the urinals was tiled to about halfway up: at first it didn't look too bad, and she thought she wouldn't need to wash it all. But once she began to scrub, the contrast between the cleaned area and the rest was just too obvious; she saw that she'd have to go over the whole lot. She squatted to get at the run of tiles between the urinals and a little gutter along the floor. The caustic fumes caught in her throat, and she pressed her nose into the sleeve of her old tracksuit top. Pam meanwhile was covering the rooms upstairs. The office workers warmed up soup in the microwave, Pam reported, and left the dirty bowls out on the desks.

There were nine or ten men at work on the warehouse floor, mostly middle-aged, all wearing blue overalls with the company logo; the forklifts trundled up and down with armfuls of the insulation wadding packed in plastic wrap for dispatch, beeping when they reversed. The younger men listened to music through headphones as they worked, which was what Shelley did too. Her MP3 player had been a Christmas present from Kerry the year before. She'd wanted at the time to give it back; she'd never have an occasion to use it, she said, and Kerry shouldn't have been spending her money on presents, anyway—she'd have enough to spend it on when the baby came.

—You're such an ungrateful cow, Kerry had said cheerfully. —Just wait and see.

Roy hadn't seemed to mind the sight of his seventeen-year-old daughter with her pregnant

27

belly swollen out like a football. Like a bomb, Kerry put it.

—She was so clever at school. I wanted her to do something better, Shelley had said. —Not just what the rest of them around here do—shelling out more kids.

—Not so clever at biology, Roy said.

—I will do something better, Kerry reassured her. —Later.

—Don't think you're going to be leaving it for me to look after. Just when I've got my own life back.

But the baby—Morgan—was so alert, twisting her head in her pushchair to follow where the conversation went, her eyes drinking everything in. She'd walked at only nine months, right from the kitchen into the living room the very first time; you had to watch her every moment.

*   *   *

When Shelley went for a fag break in the car park, she switched her phone back on for a few minutes. There was only a text from Roy, who drove a courier van—something stupid. He was always on the lookout for the funny names they gave to hairdressers' and fishmongers' and so on: A Cut Above, The Plaice to Go, that sort of thing. She supposed it passed the time.

—Anyway, I took my net curtains down, Pam said, when Shelley went through the side door into the canteen. Teabags were bobbing, leaking colour, in two mugs of milky water. —I don't know when I'll get them back up again.

—Why's that then?

28

—Didn't I tell you my washing machine's bust? The whole kitchen was flooded. John sent me a picture of it on my mobile while I was at the back of the queue in the post office—it was the last day for mail-order returns. Now I've got this pair of trousers I can't get into.

—I can't believe he just sent you the picture.

—He claimed he didn't know where I kept the mop.

Roy said that Pam had to be getting something out of her relationship with John or else she wouldn't keep on with it. Is that how it is? Shelley wondered. What we get is what we really want?

Back in the toilets, she started on the sinks. The fibrous wadding the men worked with got everywhere; it had stained the enamel orange-pink. She had to use a toothbrush to scrub where it had mixed with green soap from the dispenser, then caked in mineral crusts around the base of the taps, around the plughole and the overflow. One of the young ones hurrying in the door, hanging on to himself through his overalls, stopped short at the sight of her; she told him to use a cubicle.

—Don't go dripping on my floor, she said, —or there'll be trouble. I know what boys are like.

When Anthony was a teenager he'd been as tense as a whiplash, swaggering around with his shirt half unbuttoned and his eyebrows pierced, stinking to heaven of Lynx aftershave, hanging out with all the worst types on the estate. Even when he was a tiny boy and really did look like an angel, he'd always given her trouble. She'd had to wrestle with him just to get his clothes on in the mornings, she'd been called in to school by his teacher time and again because he was fighting or disrespectful.

29

But sometimes when Shelley dropped him off in the junior playground he'd put his finger on his cheek to show her the exact spot where he wanted her to kiss him goodbye—their little joke from when he was a baby. She and Roy had split up for a while when Anthony was eighteen months, and after they'd got back together she'd had Kerry. Anthony was the one who looked like Shelley, not how she looked now but how she used to: skinny and fair, with big hungry eyes. She hadn't been able to believe it when he'd got into the Army. She couldn't understand why they'd want a boy like him.

—They'll soon have him sorted out, she said, but actually she'd been so angry that she couldn't forgive him—or anyone else, either. She'd blamed Roy for reading war books and leaving them lying round the house. Or it was Anthony's girlfriend's fault: Leanne only wanted the money for those two kids who weren't Anthony's; she didn't care what he had to do to get it.

—He's going to make a proper career for himself, Roy said. —You ought to be proud of him, working so hard to pass his qualifications.

It wasn't that she wasn't proud of Anthony. The Army really had sorted him out: the first time he came home on leave he was tanned from training outdoors, his neck had thickened and his shoulders bulked out. He'd had his hair cropped short, and he seemed calmer and more deliberate. —I didn't do too bad, he said, his glance slipping away from his mother towards the others. He'd never done a day's hard work in his life, and now suddenly he seemed weighed down with sense and responsibility.

At first, whenever he was on leave he was keen to hang about with his old no-good friends, but

30

eventually he lost interest in them. He said they were going nowhere, smoking themselves silly, which was just what Shelley had always told him. His officers thought he was dedicated, a good soldier.

Since Anthony had been posted to Afghanistan, Roy had gone on the Internet and found out everything about what was going on there. He followed it on the blogs and on YouTube. He talked about 'the lines' and 'advance to contact' and 'hearts and minds'. Shelley thought this talk made Anthony uncomfortable, because it was impossible for him to share with them what really happened out there. He'd told them once about clearing out Taliban compounds after an attack and finding the bloody clothes they'd left behind when they retreated with their dead and wounded; it had occurred to Shelley that he must have seen much worse than bloody clothes, and then she guessed that he was describing the clothes because he couldn't talk about the other things. Whenever they parted now, he kissed her as if he were putting her aside, kindly but firmly.

She felt around in the blocked sink with her rubber gloves, poking into the plughole with the toothbrush, pulling at the ends of the fibres caught in the trap, tugging and coaxing until she began to deliver up out of the drain a nasty mass, a thick rope of hair and soap and matted insulation, in a gulp of bad drain smell. Triumphant, she flopped it out on to the enamel, black-green and slimed. The foul water, released, went gurgling down the pipe, and at that moment Shelley was washed through with one of her hot flushes. She had to stop to tear her gloves off inside out, flap her T-shirt, lift

31

her hair away from her blazing neck. She leaned forward over the sink, unexpectedly dizzy, taking her weight on her arms and staring down into the dark passage of the drain, understanding it for a few seconds as if it opened a way out of the world, or into it. Then, hearing the boy flush the toilet in the cubicle behind her, she scooped up the nasty mess with some paper towels and dropped it into the black bag she had with her for rubbish, so that he would not have to see it.

*　　　*　　　*

When the job was finished they packed away their gear; the car park was full now, but there was no one about outside. Pam struggled to start the car: she always gave it too much choke, Roy said. Shelley in the passenger seat turned on her mobile. There was a bad moment every time, while the logo appeared and the music chimed. She expected the worst then; she seemed to be staring out for it greedily, her heart straining.

—All right? Pam asked her.

The little car, after its hacking convulsions, rocked into silence, resigned.

—All right, Shelley said. —Nothing.

They sat there for a few minutes, too tired to move, giving the car time to recover, talking about their Christmas shopping: who they'd bought for, what they still had to get. More than half the short winter's day had passed while they were in the warehouse. The sky was a blue so pale that it was almost no colour; wooded bluffs loomed above them, beyond the industrial estate, marking the edge of the city. The sun had dropped behind the bluffs already, so that the tops of the bare trees showed up finely spiky, like hair or fur, against a yellow glow of light from somewhere out of sight. While they waited, their breath began to fog up the car windows.

A Mouthful of Cut Glass

The house where Neil was born, in 1952, had been at the centre of Birmingham, in a Victorian slum that was knocked down a few years later. Nobody lived there now, there were only roads and office blocks, and the people who'd lived in the slums had been moved out to the new estates that ringed the city. Neil told Sheila that the house he was born in had had a crack in the outside wall that let the rain and wind through, so that for the years he lived there he and his sister had had to sleep in his mum and dad's room, because they couldn't use the bedroom upstairs. His sister had slept in a cot until she was six; he had slept in the bed with his parents. He told Sheila that the house had shared a yard at the back with several other houses in the terrace; there were outside toilets and a brick wash-house with a coal-fired boiler and a mangle where the women did their laundry. The house had been condemned by the council the whole time he lived there, but the family had had to wait for the authorities to find them somewhere else to live.

At university in Bristol in 1972, Neil didn't have to be ashamed of these things or hide them. Because of the politics of the time, the student politics especially, his origins were even glamorous. It was the children of bankers and managing directors who had to apologise for their upbringing, and practise roughening their too refined accents. Sheila had grown up with eight brothers and sisters in a vicarage in Suffolk; vicars' daughters were in a category so impossibly quaint and comical that it hardly seemed worth despising.

Neil could have played on his working-class credentials much more than he did. Sheila had never heard him tell anyone else, for instance, about the crack in the wall. This reserve, like a strength withheld, was part of what made her love him quite desperately. He was very clever and he had absolute opinions; friends glanced quickly at him after they spoke, to see what he thought. Sheila had never expected to love someone who was two inches shorter than she was. It was a surprise to discover how her desire could attach itself to the aura of Neil's power and not to the particulars of his face and body, which in her mental picture of him were always blurred. Although he wasn't fat, he was rather soft and shapeless; his walk was shambling and he hid behind his long brown hair. When he pushed the hair back, his face was round, sweet like a girl's. Yet just the thought of the quick, small, almost prim smile that flickered open in his expression when he was amused made Sheila sick with longing; it touched her more nakedly even than when he made love to her, because he did that with irony, holding himself back.

In the autumn of her second year, Neil took her home for a weekend to meet his family. He hadn't been especially keen to do this. He'd warned her that she would be bored, that his parents would make a big fuss, but Sheila had wheedled at him until he gave way. His family didn't have a telephone; he left a message with the neighbours. She braced herself then for something dark and raw, something that differed definitively from her own past. Whenever she remembered the vicarage she felt coilings of shame at the meanness of her

35

life there. For all her family's crowded closeness, neither her parents nor her siblings were any good at intimacy; they communicated in evasive codes, fumbling and deflecting contact. She prepared a perfect openness for her visit to Neil's home, ready to offer up her real self at last. They caught a bus from the coach station out to Northfield and then walked up through the estate. Rows of low grey houses curved behind open grass spaces, their front doors all painted the same red. Children were playing in the streets. A man was cutting a hedge with shears in a front garden. The place wasn't pretty, exactly, but it was neat and respectable. This took Sheila by surprise. She realised that although she knew that Neil's family had moved out of the slums when he was a child, she had gone on imagining him pressed upon by frowning Victorian concentrations of population.

Neil seemed relaxed enough; she had been afraid that her difference might embarrass him on his home ground. She'd expected him to move more self-consciously here, where he might be known and recognised, but he didn't lift his head to look out for old friends or greet them. He must have walked these streets with the same absorption as a schoolboy, all those years when he was taking the bus seven miles every day to the grammar school in town where he'd got a free place, with the briefcase that his parents had proudly bought for him, full of the books that were going to educate him out of the estate.

—Clover Close, he said merrily. —Grassymead Lane. Oak Grove. Hazelbush Way. You'd think you were in the Forest of Arden if you closed your eyes. Except that real country addresses never sound anything like that. The test is if the name is as plain as possible, then you know it's the real thing. The ruling classes live in places called Old Hall. Stone House. Long End. The Rectory.

Sheila's home was called The Rectory and it was in the country, but nowhere like the Forest of Arden. It was in a bleak, poor village in East Anglia, where the red brick rectory was the grandest building after the church. Neil had said once that his dad, who was a tool-setter at Lucas Engineering, probably earned more than hers; she had no idea if he was right.

Neil's dad Dennis stood waiting for them in his shirtsleeves and braces at the front door, which was on the side of the house, opening on to the kitchen. He was compact and smiling, with a round face and thick peachy skin, rosy where the blood vessels were broken across his cheeks; his springy grey-black hair was slicked back with Brylcreem. He had the air of a man used to performing a comical role, pleasant and placating. When Neil's mother May came crowding behind him in the doorway, wiping her hands on a tea towel, Sheila saw that she was small too; Neil overtopped them both. Sheila was going to be the tallest person in the house.

—All right, son? Neil's father grinned at him. —You can still find your way back home, then? Which bus did you get?

He held out a disproportionately huge hand to shake Sheila's, and although he touched her with scrupulous gentleness she felt the strength in his grip. When Neil explained which bus they'd taken and how it had wound slowly around another estate for forty minutes, his father shook his head in disbelief: the eccentricity of the buses was clearly

37

an old comfortable joke. In Bristol, Neil would have scorned such small talk. May, hanging back, kept her hands wrapped in the tea towel, nodding and smiling shyly; she had a miniature figure like a doll's, with skinny little-girl legs gauche under her short skirt. Sandwiches made from sliced white bread, cut into perfect triangles, were set out on a counter on two plates, covered with paper torn from bread wrappers.

—I said not to make a fuss, Neil said to his mother, helping himself to a sandwich; May in a darting movement slapped at his hand, scolding him. —It's all right, he reassured her. —Sheila hasn't got any manners, either.

May blushed and couldn't look at Sheila. —Don't take any notice of him, she said apologetically. —I don't.

Sheila heard now that Neil's Birmingham accent, which she had thought so strong, was softened and compromised compared with the way his parents spoke.

—She'll have cooked us a meal, too, Neil warned. —This is just to tide us over.

—I thought after your journey you'd want something. Shall I put the kettle on for tea?

The kitchen was too small to sit down in so Neil and Sheila drank their tea on a sofa in the living room, in front of the gas fire turned up high. Sheila was so eager to please that she ate all the sandwiches on her plate, though she didn't know how she was going to manage anything else. The shoebox-shaped room was a little gem of neatness. There were antimacassars along the back of the sofa and on the back of every chair, a glass-fronted cabinet full of ornaments, framed photographs on

38

the tiled mantelpiece of Neil and his sister Chris, of Chris's wedding. Neil had told Sheila that every Friday after his mother came back from her job at the bakery she stacked the furniture and rolled up all the carpets to wash the floor underneath.

—Are you at the college with our Neil then, Sheila? his father asked. Sheila was surprised that Neil hadn't told them more about her. She didn't talk to her parents much, but she was sure that they knew at least where Neil came from and what subject he was reading.

She explained that she was reading classics, Latin and Greek.

—Very interesting, Dennis said. —*Veni, vidi, vici.*

—All that stuff. It's the Greeks that I love. Revenge and passion, the war between the sexes, justice on earth. Of course, it'll be no use to anyone after I've finished, but I don't care. My dad read classics, too, so it's in the family, I suppose.

—It's brewing that's in mine, Neil's mother said with a quick laugh. Sheila knew that May's uncle and brothers worked at Davenports the brewers; they had got Neil a job there over the summer.

Neil ate only a couple of sandwiches, then he got out his cigarettes.

—Go on, have one of mine, son, his mother said, pushing a pack of Embassy Regals at him. —Do you smoke, Sheila?

Sheila didn't. But she saw the moment of closeness it made between mother and son, heads bent together over the lighter, eyes narrowed and cheeks hollowed in inhalation. May had a little chrome-and-Formica smoking table at her end of the sofa, with an ashtray fixed in the centre on a metal stalk. Although Neil's face was round like his father's, the wary sharpness in it made him resemble his mother more. Like Neil, May glanced evasively sideways at whoever she was speaking to. In his teenage years, Sheila knew, Neil's mother had been his confidante, talking late into the night with him and his friends when he brought them home. She seemed more assured with the cigarette in her hand; a social manner descended on her, mildly rakish and teasing.

—I tried to get him to put something decent on, because you were coming. May nodded at her husband. —But he goes his own way.

—She's not bothered, Dennis said. —Are you, Sheila?

—I'm so glad you didn't. Sheila smiled at them. —Look at us. We're a real mess. We don't want you to do anything different from what you do usually. Please.

She wondered what they thought of her clothes, a long crimson Indian skirt with braid around the hem and a crushed-velvet top embroidered with mirrors: these might be their idea of disgraceful rags. She hoped that her looks worked for her, though: her pale skin and long curling red-brown hair. She knew that Dennis was paying her subtle, harmless attentions because of them, without even knowing that he was doing it: spooning sugar into her tea and smoothing the creases out of her coat when he hung it up.

—You're right about Neil. He is a right mess. What about that hair? What does he think he looks like? Dennis broke out suddenly.

—Oh, leave him alone, May said. —Why shouldn't he have it how he wants? That's how they all wear it now.

40

Neil smiled to himself: that private irrepressible smile of his, as if he couldn't help being delighted at some comedy he was watching. Dennis didn't seem to mean his complaint to offend anyone. He was a joker, an entertainer. You could see that he was the one to confront the public world, sheltering May, who had been brought up in an orphanage after her mother died and her father abandoned the family. Dennis took care to mention this more than once, as if the injustice of it still rankled with him.

—Sheila lives in a rectory, Neil offered. —Her dad's a vicar in Suffolk.

—That's nice, May said.

Sheila wanted to tell them about the rectory: how it was actually cold and bare and full of worn, scuffed furniture, not nearly as comfortable as this cosy room. But she didn't because she was afraid they wouldn't believe her, and would think that she was patronising them, trying to put them at ease because she found their home so poor.

May and Dennis got out photographs from a coach trip they had taken to Scotland. Before university, Neil had gone with them on these trips. He had explained to Sheila how, now that so many holidaymakers were going abroad, the big old country hotels that had once been exclusively for the wealthy had begun to cater to working-class coach parties. She tried to imagine Neil spending his days with a coachload of middle-aged Brummies, set apart by his youth and education, flirted with by the older women, thinking his own thoughts, taking an informed interest in all the places they visited. She found the idea seductive. He had certainly travelled more widely in Britain than she ever had, and knew more about its history.

41

In the photographs Dennis was usually at the centre, posed against some monument or other. Sheila was surprised that he and May relished so uncritically the grand style of their holiday: the food, the thick carpets, the ballrooms, the chandeliers, the free whisky at the distillery tour, the free soap in the bathrooms. She had expected that they would despise the luxuries of the rich, as she and Neil did. She felt a mixture of relief and deflation, as if she'd been cheated of something she'd braced herself to take on: some intensity of engagement, both scorching and testing. This is going to be easy, she thought. After all, they're just easy sweet people.

*   *   *

They put Sheila in Chris's old bedroom, in a bed made up with nylon sheets and the same rough old army blankets her mother had at home. There wasn't much evidence of Chris left in the room: a framed embroidered picture of a squirrel, a hollow soapstone swan with a couple of hair grips in it on the dressing table. May assured Sheila that there was plenty of hot water because the immersion heater had been on all evening, but although Sheila rather longed for a bath, she didn't want to keep everybody waiting for the bathroom. She cleaned her teeth quickly. Everything in here was scoured spotless. The only difference between May's cheap thin towels and bath mat and the ones at home was that these had been cherished and ironed.

Sheila undressed and slithered down between cold sheets, then lay awake listening to the life of the house subside—low-voiced exchanges of practicalities, the sound of a bolt being shot to. She imagined that she was hearing what Neil had heard all his life before he came to Bristol. She was in that phase of the relationship where everything associated with Neil seemed to her charged with excitement, even the smell of the clothes he took off and left lying on the floor, even his favourite tracks on albums that she would never have chosen for herself, Grateful Dead and Captain Beefheart. She couldn't sleep. After a while, when everything was quiet, she pushed back the sheets and knelt on the bed in her nightdress, looking out of the window at the orange sodium lights and a flare of fire somewhere, perhaps from a factory chimney. Nearby she could make out the silhouetted dome of the lunatic asylum, which Neil had pointed out when he showed her the room—built in the nineteenth century in what had then been countryside. The air was chilly on her shoulders. The little house seemed to drop very quickly into cold once the gas fire was out, as if the walls were only a thin skin between the night and the lives inside.

She pressed down the handle on the bedroom door very carefully, then crept along the landing, trying not to make any sound on the lino with her bare feet. She knew which room was Neil's—she had looked into it earlier and seen his few books on a shelf, the only books in the house, and the old card table where he had done his homework for all those years. She slipped inside and soundlessly closed the door behind her. Neil reared up in bed; in the light from the street lamps she could see the mound of the blankets around his shoulders. Sheila cuddled quickly in beside him. She had let herself get thoroughly chilled, sitting looking out the window; now the heat of his body against hers under the blankets was like a flood. To her surprise he was wearing pyjamas, which he never did in Bristol; they smelled of his mother's washing.

He hissed a protest at her frozen feet. —What are you doing? he whispered in perplexity, grasping her by the shoulder. —We can't do that here.

—I can't sleep, she complained. —I miss you.

She pressed herself close against the length of him, kissing his neck and his ears, trying to undo his pyjama buttons. He pushed her off.

—Sh-h-h. You can hear everything in this house. They'll know.

—We could be so quiet.

—No.

—Then just let me sleep here. I'll go back in the morning.

—They'll know. Honestly. Believe me.

—OK. Let me stay for ten minutes.

To show that he was sorry he kissed her then, but warily, not wanting to be carried away into anything. Their mouths tasted of meat from May's casserole, which Sheila had eaten even though she was a vegetarian. With her lips she felt the growth of beard on Neil's jawbone, not bristling but silky; he was giving out his kisses one by one, sceptically, like a bird pecking. This tension of thwarted longing—even when they were on their own and could do whatever they liked—was somehow the whole character of their relationship. Sheila was always frantic for the next thing she didn't have from Neil; the sensation was as painful as wire spooled taut in her chest. She wondered sometimes

44

what would become of them if the spool gave way and the tension slackened. After a while he stopped kissing her, and she knew that he really wasn't going to let her stay.

On the landing on the way back to her room, she heard May and Dennis talking in their bedroom. That was good, it meant that they weren't lying awake listening to her move about. She took a couple of cautious steps and stood where she might be able to catch what they were saying. She had never had any compunction about eavesdropping, or reading other people's letters or diaries; at home, with so many brothers and sisters, a certain level of surveillance had been almost necessary for survival—unless you sneaked, you never learned what was going on. Anyway, she trusted herself to understand whatever she found out.

She couldn't really hear May and Dennis. May was angry about something, Dennis was soothing her: he rumbled, reasonable, sympathetic. They were both suppressing their voices, naturally, in this house of thin walls. May's tone was different from the one she'd used all evening: hard and final. Sheila knew at once that this must be her real voice, the one she used with people she was comfortable with.

—How can I talk to her? Sheila heard May say then, quavering suddenly louder. —With that accent like a mouthful of cut glass?

Sheila's heart heaved: the thud was so strong she even imagined that Dennis and May had heard it, until he rumbled again and she knew she was safe. It serves you right, she told herself immediately, not knowing quite what it was that she had deserved, or what for.

45

Back in bed, she lay huddled with her knees pulled up inside her nightdress, the taste of the casserole meat rising from her stomach. She was going over the work that she had to do for the following week: a Latin prose translation, an essay on *Medea*. But just as she fell into sleep she recognised that May had muddled two quite separate expressions. How stupid, Sheila thought. It has to be either 'talking through a mouthful of plums' or 'an accent like cut glass'. Not 'a mouthful of cut glass'. She's made nonsense of it.

For a moment, however, she could imagine the sensation of chewing politely and sufferingly on a mouthful of broken crystal, tasting salty blood.

*　　　*　　　*

Neil came to the rectory for a few days after Christmas. Sheila never quite got over the surprise of his being there, where he didn't belong, among the left-behind scenes of her childhood. She knew that she was reacting badly to the situation—as if she were blinking into a light that distracted her from seeing him fairly. She was irritated when he seemed to get along with her parents. At supper the first night, he talked with her father about the Knox family; Sheila's family—the Culverts—was distantly related to them. A Culvert had been one of the first Evangelical bishops to be ordained in the Church of England: the old sober kind of Evangelical, not the new guitar-playing excitable kind. Neil knew about the Ronald Knox translation of the Bible because his mother had been brought up a Catholic, and because he knew about so many things. Reverend Culvert told him about the Roman earthenware

46

found in the scrubland close to the river that the villagers called the Ditch, and about the carved flints that lay about in the fields for picking up. He sputtered mashed potato and gesticulated with pleasure at having someone informed to talk to. His own children kept their intellectual interests strictly apart from family mealtimes; they were embarrassed if their father ever veered from his habitual ironic distance. He was a tall thin man, whose head with its long earlobes was austere in repose, as if it were carved out of hard ancient wood; to see him so boyishly eager was compromising, like watching a tortoise bob its skinny neck out from the decency of its shell.

Sheila was aware of how gratifying it was to her father that someone like Neil, who came from a working-class background, should be doing so well. The Reverend, despite the disappointments he was daily faced with—the sullen village boys, their cursing, their fatalism—kept up, in the solitude of his study at least, a whole set of hopeful ideals that had to do with justice and progress. Sheila winced when he gleamed with pleased surprise at Neil's intelligent comments. She and her siblings had grown up with a horror that their father might sometime make a sermon out of the things that they did, or that happened to them. Sheila's mother, peculiar and ravaged, was simply grateful that the conversation didn't require her dutiful bolstering; she bowed her head low over her plate to eat, while the children exchanged veiled glances. The boys were horrible mimics: they would be mentally rehearsing Neil's accent. The gammon was too salty and the parsley sauce had been made from a packet; Sheila only ate the mash and the

Brussels sprouts. Her mother's cooking was loveless and institutional. An old book of fine recipes in French—a wedding present—sat unopened on a shelf above the kitchen stove, its pages gummed together by the steam from hundreds of pans of boiling potatoes.

—How can you not see how awful they are? Sheila hissed to Neil the next day when she took him on a walk to get away from the house. They set out along the flank of the wide shallow valley, into a freezing wind that rippled the slate-coloured water standing on the clay in the valley bottom, where the Ditch had overflowed. —They're so dried up, so false. Nothing they say is ever real.

He shrugged. —At least your parents don't make remarks about West Indians being too lazy to work and wanting to sit all day with a string tied round their big toe, fishing in the creek.

—I wish they would, Sheila said gloomily. —Does your dad really believe that?

—Didn't he treat you to his Al Jolson impression?

—But don't you see how sickening the opposite thing is, too? Always having to be up on the moral high ground. We actually have a family abbreviation for it, you know: the MHG. Mum shouts it when the kids are quarrelling: 'MHG! Back down and take the MHG!' Sometimes the whole family goes berserk—I can't tell you. My brother Andrew—the one who left home—once stabbed Stephen with a fork. He was shouting at him, 'Cunt, cunt, cunt!' Dad was trying to separate them, Mum was threatening to call the police. Then that evening when it had all died down we were just sitting around the table again, eating boiled liver or

48

something, pretending that nothing had happened. 'Almighty God, who hast given us grace at this time.'

Neil laughed.

—You closed your eyes when he prayed at the table last night, she said accusingly.

—Did I? No, I didn't.

Sheila was walking backward ahead of him along the path, in her eagerness to convey to him the truth about her parents. The wind on her back whipped her hair across her face from under her knitted hat. Mrs Culvert had insisted that Neil, who didn't own a hat, borrow some awful thing from the tallboy in the hall which no one could remember ever wearing, a kind of bonnet with a furry lining and earflaps; it changed him piquantly, into a beady-eyed, perky cartoon animal. He seemed more interested in the landscape than in Sheila's family. He asked her the names of places they could see, which she didn't always know; he couldn't believe that she had lived here all her life and wasn't sure where north was. They reached a stand of beech trees growing on a slope about a mile from the village. Among the trees, the wind that had blown so insistently against them dropped, and they stopped to recover their equilibrium on a muffling carpet of dried leaves. The smooth trunks of the trees surging up out of the earth seemed present and intelligent, grey beasts standing soberly to watch them. A musky mushroomy perfume rose in the stillness from the mulch underfoot. Neil put his arms around Sheila and kissed her; the embrace felt comical and unsexual through their bulky layers of jumpers, coats and scarves.

—I could put my coat on the ground, Neil said

49

insinuatingly into her neck, his earflaps scratching her chin. —It would be nice to cuddle up.

—You're joking, Sheila said in horror. —In broad daylight?

Needless to say, at the rectory they were sleeping separately: Sheila was in her old room with her sister Hilary, Neil was in with Anthony and Stephen. —I feel awful, Mrs Culvert had mumbled, not looking at Neil, bobbing her thick shock of grey hair and apologising for there being no spare room that he could have to himself. —What you must think . . . Of course we should—five bedrooms. Don't know if Sheila's told you Gillian's problems? (Gillian, who was eight, was epileptic, and had difficulty coping with school. She was seeing a psychiatrist in Cambridge; apparently she needed her own room. 'Which makes me think she's smarter than she looks,' Sheila had said.)

—We're out in the countryside, Neil said to Sheila, nuzzling her. —There's no one to see.

—That just shows how much you know about the countryside. She pushed him away from her with both gloved hands. —Everyone will know that we're up here already. If we don't walk on soon, they'll be looking at their watches.

—Who cares? he said, trying again.

—I do, she said passionately. —Don't spoil this place for me. It's somewhere I used to come to be by myself when I was a girl, when I couldn't bear any of them at home. It's holy to me. I used to read poetry here.

Neil couldn't argue with that, and so they moved on, faintly mutually resentful long after they'd resumed holding hands and talking. In fact, Sheila had somewhat misrepresented the significance of the beech grove. She had used to go there with Hilary; she would never have gone walking anywhere around here on her own. It was true, though, that she and her sister had sometimes brought their books to the grove with them, and had worked themselves up over what they were reading into states of exalted excitement.

When they had all eaten their cauliflower cheese that evening, Mrs Culvert suggested unexpectedly that they play games.

—We always do at Christmas, she explained to Neil. —Family tradition . . . no television. With you here—new blood, so to speak.

Neil was fairly appalled at the idea and no one else seemed keen, but nonetheless when the washing up was done they assembled to play in the front room, the girls snuggling round the meek warmth of the storage heater with their jumpers pulled down over their hands, the boys erupting into spasms of kicking on the broken-backed sofa. Mrs Culvert carried armfuls of props downstairs for charades and dumped them triumphantly in a heap: a fur coat, a parasol, straw boaters, an inflatable rubber ring for the beach, an air-raid warden's helmet, dog leashes, an evening dress of crinkled green Fortuny silk, a croquet mallet. The Reverend, in magnanimous concession, poured glasses of fizzy cider for everyone but the three youngest children.

Poor Neil was out of his depth. He had never played charades before, and he was hopeless at it. His team acted 'Eucharist', and for 'ewe' they dressed him up as a shepherd in a stripy flannelette sheet with a crook left over from someone's Nativity play. Nola and Patricia frisked around his feet, baaing, while Hilary who was usually earnest

51

and silent followed on all fours, wrapped in a sheepskin rug from the study. Neil made no effort to get into the role of the shepherd; he batted uncomfortably at the girls with his crook and almost ruined everything by mumbling pointedly, —And here's the ewe, when Hilary appeared.

The Culverts threw themselves into these games, once they got started, with an extravagance that was almost a mania. For 'wrist', Reverend Culvert put on the green silk dress and minced up and down with his wife's handbag, drooping his wrist and exclaiming, —Dear me, ducky. Neil looked frankly astonished. He wasn't much better at guessing, either. Hilary and her father got Sheila's team's word—'seductress'—long before Neil did; they held back to give him a chance, and he stared miserably, bemusedly, at Mrs Culvert's egg-laying (—Poultry? he ventured), and at Stephen as a hairdresser perming Anthony's blond nylon wig. Sheila, acting the whole word in the finale, in her father's silk dressing gown and a pair of old high heels, was languidly seductive as Neil had never seen her: husky-voiced, rolling her hips, adjusting her stocking, letting the dressing gown fall open when she sat down, smoothing her perfectly shaped long legs. She patted a place beside her on the sofa for her mother, dressed as a shy boy, in tails with a top hat and cane, a moustache drawn with a black mascara brush on her upper lip; she pulled the boy over by his tie to kiss her. Neil was dismayed to feel strong stirrings of desire as he watched.

—Never mind! Mrs Culvert said to him consolingly when the game was over and they all sat flushed and panting among the disregarded heaps of costumes and props, bubbling weakly with smiles and shamed giggles at what they had done. Mrs Culvert still had her moustache. —Awfully silly, really, she said. —You'll get the hang of it next time.

*　　　*　　　*

The next morning, Sheila and Hilary took the short cut through the garden on their way back from buying hair dye at the shop in the village; Sheila was determined to do something with Hilary's mousy hair. The short cut meant that they had to plough through dead weeds and brambles at the long garden's bottom end. A wet mist like sticky, grubby wool was still clinging to the earth at ten o'clock, and their trousers were almost immediately soaked to the knees, the water seeping through their desert boots to their socks. They tugged at the naked branches of a silver birch overhead to drench each other thoroughly, squealing in the shower of drops. For the first time, Sheila experienced a rush of strong feeling for her home and her past, a tenderness for the winter garden's desolation. The same grey sodden dishcloths had been left hanging for months on the washing line. A plastic bucket was half filled with rotting apples from the trees. Children's trikes and an old pedal car had been left out to rot too. Everything in the flower beds had over-grown and died, and now the silky seed heads and swollen blackened pods, slashed down by wind and rain, lay dissolving into the earth.

The daylight was so grudging that the lamp was turned on in the vicar's study. The sisters had often watched their father from out here as he rehearsed his sermons or conducted symphonies on the gramophone, thinking nobody could see him. Neil had found some LPs that Andrew had left behind, and Reverend Culvert, who was visiting elderly parishioners in hospital this morning, had said at breakfast that he could play them in the study if he wanted to. Through the French windows, the girls could see him sitting cross-legged on the floor, smoking, his hair falling forward across his face. He was swaying his head in time to a song they couldn't hear: rock music, Frank Zappa probably, nothing that the dusty old study with its walls of books had ever been treated to before. (Andrew had had his own hi-fi, which he had taken away with him.) Hilary couldn't help bursting out with a snort of laughter.

—I'm sorry, Shuggs, but he does look funny.

—It's all right, Sheila said. —I know he does.

She was taken aback by this stranger of hers, ensconced so outrageously in the innermost sanctum of her family home. The shock of it was voluptuous; she felt with a shudder that the closer Neil came to her, the less familiar he was. She would have liked to see her life as he saw it, stripped of its ordinariness; she wished that she could possess him as he only was when he was alone. She heard a soft thud and a rattle of glass; Neil heard it too from inside the room, and turned his head. Hilary had picked out one of the tiny half-rotten apples from the bucket and pitched it at the study windows, dropping to hide herself behind a stretch of overgrown wall where there had once been a greenhouse. When Neil looked away again, she stood up to pitch another one; Sheila joined in. Neil got to his feet. It must have been difficult, with the light on, for him to see them in the murky

54

day outside. He came over and peered through the French windows and they threw apples at him, not bothering in the end to hide, standing out in the grey daylight as he watched them, hurling all the apples at him, one after another, until they reached a layer of impossibly mushy ones at the very bottom of the bucket.

The Trojan Prince

It's an April morning and a young man waits at a black-painted front door in a decent street in Tynemouth. It's a much more decent street than the one where his home is. Both streets are terraced, but here the scale's quite different; a curving flight of stone steps climbs to the door, flanked by railings also painted black. Dropped behind more railings there's a basement area, and rising from down there are the sounds of pans clashing and women's voices, and the steam of cooking—but he's determinedly not looking down. He fixes his attention on the front door as if he's willing it to open—he has tugged at the bell-pull and heard a distant jangling inside, but doesn't know if he'll have the nerve to pull it twice. The year is 1920. This young man has missed the World War—he has closed his mind now even to the idea of the war, which, it seems to him, has devoured everyone's pity and imagination for too long.

The street is quiet. It's past the hour when the kind of men who live in these houses leave for their offices and boardrooms—he has meant to avoid them. But he's hoping it's still early enough for the women to be at home. He has only a vague idea of how the kind of women who live here pass their days. The wind is tearing scraps of cloud in a fitfully gleaming sky, and combing through the twigs of the hornbeam trees (the trees are another difference between this street and his), setting them springing and dancing like whips. Last night it rained heavily—he lay awake listening to it in the

56

bed he shares with his brother—and the stone walls are still dark with wet, though the wind has dried the pavements. Beside the door an iron implement something like the upside-down end of a hoe is set into the stone step; too late, just as the door swings back, he realises that it must be for scraping the mud off your boots before you go inside the house. He's walked or run down this street a hundred times before, and never noticed the boot scrapers or given any thought to their function, because then he was a boy with no interest in going inside. There's no time now to check whether his boots are dirty.

A maid has opened the door—he knew that would happen and worried that she might be a girl he'd known at school. But she's a stranger, tall and big-boned with a smut on her cheek, so he's able to push past her into the hall, doffing his cap. It's only as the still atmosphere of the house envelops him that he's aware of the particular weather of the morning left behind—its touch on his face and tug at his coat, the urgings of the onset of spring, the twigs glowing russet, swelling into bud.

—Can I speak to Miss Ellen, please? he says, with the aplomb he has rehearsed at home.

The cessation of the wind is so abrupt that he feels for a moment as if he were deaf; it must be the quiet that makes this house seem so different to his own, because the smells are familiar enough: furniture polish, scalded dish-rags, boiling cabbage. The maid is frowning at him sulkily, not knowing if she should have let him in. He guesses that she spends her life afraid of trouble from one side or another.

—Don't know if she's at home.

—I should think she'd like to see me. She'll be sorry if she misses me. I'm her cousin. I'm going away to sea.

The maid dithers fatalistically.

—I'll go and tell Missus. What's your name?

—McIlvanney, he says. —Tell her it's James McIlvanney.

—Do you want to wait here, then?

—Here's all right.

She puts out her hand to him and he waits a moment too long, not knowing what she wants. Then blushing he gives her his cap and sees a little light of contempt come into her eyes, which are round and hard and wet like blue pebbles—but it doesn't matter, he's got this far. Going up the stairs, she makes a show of stamping her feet heavily, as if she's actually too weary to climb to the first floor.

He's only sixteen, despite the man's overcoat and the new tweed cap. His hair is jet black and very straight, and his face is composed of strong fine lines, clean and clear and exquisite like his clear pink and white skin; his eyebrows are as well-shaped as a woman's, his curved lips pressed shut as if he's holding in important news. The jut of his cheekbones and jaw is masculine enough—strained and resilient; his expression is keenly alive with self-interest, which makes him appear blind and alert at the same time. The air in the hall is thick and dim and greenish because the blinds are all drawn down—as they are in the parlour at home—to save the light fading the furniture. It makes him remember floating underwater once, when he dived into the canal and hit his head on an old bedstead dumped in there. A clock ticking in the hall is like his own pulse urging him on. He

58

can hear the maid's voice upstairs, other voices responding, impatient, querulous—he has dropped an interruption into the smooth unfurling of the women's morning. Without warning, he experiences a slight nausea and dizziness.

He holds his head back warily, defiantly on his shoulders, so that the furnishings in here won't get the better of him: the dado with its raised pattern of diamonds under thick brown paint, the polished wood of the hall stand glowing dark, yellow gleams of brass among the shadows—the face of the clock, a rack for letters, a little gong hanging in a frame with a suede-covered mallet balanced across two hooks, a tall brass pot for the umbrellas. He doesn't look down at the pattern of blue and cream tiles underfoot in case he has trodden mud on them. Through an open door he glimpses low chairs fat with stuffing, crouched on a sea of flower-patterned carpet. The smell of brushed carpets tickles in his nose. Everything in this house is slick with prosperity, with the labour of servants. In his own home, there's only a girl who comes in two mornings a week to help his mother with the heavy work.

What James McIlvanney thinks is: I'll have all this one day.

He doesn't particularly like it, but he wants it.

He stores it up, so that he knows what to want.

But there's no definite plan of how to get it. It wasn't a plan that brought him here today. Ellen Pearson really is his cousin—second cousin, at least. She belongs to the branch of his family who have done well for themselves; his mother's uncle, Ellen's grandfather, made money in India, then came home to set up a company importing jute.

59

Ellen's mother is related to the Fenwicks, who own a department store in Newcastle. Ellen's a pale blonde girl James has seen on a couple of family occasions but never spoken to, attractive in a sickly kind of way, and shy; though the truth is, that when he last saw her at a family party he didn't bother to notice whether she was attractive or not, because then he was only a boy, chafing in his prickling wool suit, consumed by the idea of escaping to his cronies out on the streets, whose adventures at that point of his life absorbed him wholly. But since leaving school and getting a proper job, he has begun to open his eyes to the world from this altered perspective, and has found himself interested in Ellen, attributing a kind of mystery to her and her blonde languor, to the life he imagines she leads as a privileged only child.

He hasn't said a word to his mother about coming here.

All he had in mind was that Ellen would be a useful friend to have. He hasn't followed this through into any idea of paying court to her or advancing himself in the world that way; he doesn't like to think about courtship or marrying at all— and he really may be going away to sea soon. His mother wanted him to settle in his job in the office at a local boatyard, where they make the pleasure boats that run up and down the coast. But he's persuaded her to let him sign up for an indentured apprenticeship with the Prince Line, which runs cargoes across the Atlantic to South America—coal out, grain home—and up the western seaboard of America and Canada. He had to borrow money from his grandmother, for the fifty-pound deposit.

There's someone coming downstairs now. It's

not the maid—he can still hear her yapping. And he knows that it's not Mrs Pearson either, because women that age move loudly, rustling their skirts or clearing their throats. James has his back to the stairs, he's gazing at the hall stand. He refuses to look round. His neck is stiff with the awareness of subtle, furtive movements behind him—a slithering, a creaking. He thinks it must be Ellen, creeping down to take a look at who he is. Let her look, he thinks. It isn't a bad feeling. He gives himself up to her looking, with straight shoulders.

—Jimmy Mac, someone says in a teasing, gloating voice. —What are you doing here?

Caught out, he spins round to confront whoever it is.

It's a girl—not Ellen, too dark and too small. She's grinning, peering out at him from between the banisters, sitting on the stairs as if she's come shuffling down them on her backside.

It's Connie Chappell.

Because he can only see one narrow stripe of her face, it has taken him a moment to recognise her—and also because she's changed. She's had her hair chopped off and waved. She seems to be wearing some kind of pink silky pyjamas—the last thing he would have expected in this house, and halfway through the morning too. He's washed through with disapproval like strong, tarry medicine, furious that Connie is here before him, spoiling things. He remembers now hearing that Ellen had taken a shine to Connie, that there was talk of Connie moving in with the Pearsons as some kind of companion to their daughter. He must have disregarded this, because he couldn't take seriously anything to do with Connie. She isn't even properly

61

related to Ellen—only through his own family, on his father's side.

Connie is four years older than James, though she doesn't look it. When he was a baby, apparently, she used to wheel him in a pram. He believes he can dimly remember being pushed across rough grass, standing up at the front of the pram, holding on to the hood with both hands. Didn't he go flying out when the pram hit a rock? Anyway, he can't bear to think about it now, at this moment in the Pearsons' hall. There had been something consecrated about his mission to this house, as if it might mark a kind of turning point for him—but Connie's presence has punctured that mystery.

—I came to see Ellen, he says.

—Did you now? And what's all this about you going away to sea?

She is laughing at him, as if she didn't believe him. When she stands up, hanging on to the banister rail, she stretches one leg out along it like a dancer, pointing her toes and yawning. He sees that the soles of her bare feet are dirty. She's like a cat, James thinks. A sloppy little cat. Under the neat-fitting cap of her new hair, her face is intensely familiar—small and precise like a muzzle, freckled and snub-nosed, the brows exclamation points, always slightly raised.

—Come on then, she says. —If you want to see her. Ellen and me are getting dressed upstairs.

—Where's Mrs Pearson?

—Oh, somewhere about, I expect.

Connie is casually indifferent.

—You can help us decide what to put on. I know—we'll blindfold you. We'll blindfold you with

62

a stocking. Then we're going out to walk round the shops. You can come out with us. Why aren't you at work—are you on holiday? Did you take a holiday, just to come and see Ellen?

James hates the feeling she knows everything about him. The lace curtains thickly shrouding the window on the stairs suddenly seem stifling—he wants to fight through them, to get to air.

*   *   *

He has sisters, but they are older than he is and both married now. Even when they were at home, they would never have been dangling around in their nightclothes at eleven in the morning; they would have been at work for hours already, in the kitchen or turning out the lodgers' rooms, with their sleeves rolled up and coarse aprons tied over their clothes. He has never been anywhere like Ellen Pearson's bedroom before. Heavy curtains are still pulled across the windows and the beds aren't made. The air is musky as if the girls have been spraying scent, and there's a stuffy smell too, from the crumpled sheets and bodies hot from sleep. The water in a basin is scummed with soap. Ellen is standing to look at her reflection where one curtain has been dragged back to let the light in, mirror held up in one hand and a swansdown puff in the other. Motes of her face powder spin in a yellow beam of sunshine. She cries out when James steps into the room, letting the mirror fall on to the thick Turkey carpet, where it doesn't break. There's another mirror set in the door of a massive wardrobe, its bevelled edge reflecting darts of light around the papered walls. Ellen is taller and heavier than he remembered, though she

63

is only seventeen, not as old as Connie. Her apricot-coloured wrap is trimmed with lace flounces. As James takes her in, the beam of light is extinguished abruptly, clouds cover the sun outside.

He would never have come up if he'd known it was their bedroom. He was thinking Connie was going to show him into some sort of upstairs drawing room: who knew how they arranged the rooms in a house like this, with so many to spare?

—Jimmy called to see you, says Connie, coming in behind him.

Ellen is blushing; she pleads with her. —But we're not ready!

—I only came to say goodbye, he says. In his big boots, he's afraid he's going to step on one of the silky scarves and dresses and undergarments lying around as if the girls have dropped them wherever they took them off.

There was something significant and teasing in the way that Connie announced him. He wasn't confident, waiting downstairs, that Ellen would remember who he was. Now the intimation flies at him true as an arrow: she not only remembers him, she likes him. She could not have been expecting him to call—and yet he feels now that he has come because the girls conjured him up, talking about him. He's certain that they've talked about him.

—Ready for what? says Connie. —Anyway, I said we'd blindfold him. That way everything's decent—he can't see, he can only guess.

—Goodbye? Ellen asks anxiously. —Why, where are you going?

*   *   *

It's always the same—although the visits to the Pearson house are his own idea, he feels the girls are drawing him there, as though he were under their spell. After that first time, they insist he comes again, whenever he can: on his afternoons off from work, and on Sundays. When he isn't with them, he can't help remembering, though it makes him ashamed, how he sat with his back to the girls in the bedroom while they dressed, sweating in his heavy suit, Connie's white stocking wrapped twice around his eyes and tied behind his head. Ellen hadn't wanted to agree to the game; it was typical of Connie's mischief. He could taste the stale-sweetish trace of her foot's perspiration in the stocking.

Connie reminds him of the girls at school who fussed over him and derided him when he was a pretty child—girls with hard hands and mocking raucous voices, fat floppy bows in their hair. He prefers to think about his growing familiarity with the heavy furniture in the Pearson house, setting him apart from the other boys in the boatyard as if it already belonged to him. When on Sundays James sometimes crosses paths in the house with Ellen's father, he's surprised for a moment, as if Mr Pearson were the usurper in *his* domain. Mr Pearson—stooped, unsmiling, his face grey with ulcer pain—always stops to ask after James's mother. He probably thinks James is coming there for Connie.

Ellen is better-looking than Connie really—statuesque and slow and kind. Some days her skin looks doughy, with dimples like dirty fingerprints, but on other days James appreciates the golden ringlets against her white shoulders, poignant shadows in the neck of her blouse. She looks like a girl leaning on a classical pillar in a soap advertisement. Beside her, Connie is a little scamp, with her cropped hair and no figure to speak of. Connie wants Ellen to cut her hair too and they discuss it for hours. Ellen daren't, she's too afraid of her father. (James learns that Mrs Pearson's nothing to be afraid of—she's nervous, with puffy pink skin, and reads novels in her room. James weighs in against Ellen cutting her hair, he's full of scorn for Connie's cheap and showy gesture. A woman should have her reserves of hair, to uncoil at some important moment; although, if he tries to imagine the uncoiling, he feels clammy. But he admires Ellen's qualities, her low voice, her clear pronunciation, her skills at the piano, playing selections from light opera. Not that he knows anything about opera.

He tells his mother that he has called to see Ellen Pearson.

—You never did.

—Guess who I met there?

He realises he's only raised the subject so that he can use Connie's name in his mouth and spit it out. She is his enemy, he thinks.

—It was good of the Pearsons to take her in, his mother says. —Poor motherless kid.

Connie's mother was James's pa's cousin Rose; she died of a growth in her inside, after nine children. James can remember his Auntie Rose smoking while she made bread, the long ash on the end of her cigarette falling off into the dough. She was small and skinny like Connie, but very strong— she could knead enough dough at one time to bake eight loaves. —Gives the bread a bit of a flavour, she said to him, as if everything was a joke. The whole tribe of the McIlvanneys are feckless, his mother says.

*   *   *

The two girls pet James and tease him as if he is a pretty, comical doll. When he takes them out on the street, one on each arm, done up in their bell dresses and tunic suits, their tam-o'-shanters pulled at jaunty angles, everyone looks at them. Sometimes they catch the electric train into Newcastle to walk around. They talk across him, discussing clothes—'a blouse of violet georgette with beadwork . . . a sand-coloured cashmere frock with a tiered chiffon collar . . . a three-piece outfit in rose and blue tricot-silk'. It's like listening to the sailors gibbering in their foreign languages. James has to keep squinting and staring ahead—looking out for where they're going, dodging the trams and broken pavings and bicycles and horse muck—so as not to be drawn into the talk and made ridiculous. He feels as if the girls are water swirling around him while he tries to stand up straight.

There's a delay with his travelling down to Dartmouth to take up his apprenticeship. He needs another fifty pounds to buy his seagoing outfit. Connie says she doesn't believe he's actually going, but he doesn't deign to show her his signed papers. He sees that Ellen suffers when he talks about how he wants to get away from England and see the world. They take a picnic to Heaton Park and she brings a hamper with compartments for all the food and utensils, blue leather straps with little buckles holding the cups and forks and bottle opener in place. James carries it along proudly. The earth under the trees is springy leaf mould, and flowers seem to hover like a blue mist at the level of his calves. He's giddy for a moment, wading into the blue, treading down the fleshy stems of the flowers under his boots. The girls can't believe that he hasn't heard of bluebells or ever noticed them before. James is teetotal but the two girls drink wine and he's aware of their two personalities changing and loosening under its influence. They laugh and squeal more loudly, showing off. Connie likes reminding him that she's a grown-up woman and he's only a boy; she exchanges sly glances with Ellen and claims there are things he doesn't understand. They pretend they're tired, they make him lie down, then they rest their heads against his jacket, one on either side. While they close their eyes he keeps very still, watching the sky above the treetops, the clouds drifting past.

Ellen's hair seems to give off a faint smell he doesn't like—it's naphthalene from mothballs. He can tell she's not really asleep by the way she holds her head so tense and awkward against his ribs. Connie is mumbling and nuzzling into his breast, dribbling, until he pushes her off and she rolls over with her back to him, in a knot with her knees drawn up. At his Auntie Rose's, when they were kids, he and his brothers were put to sleep in Connie's bedroom once or twice. He remembers Connie in her vest and knickers, her skinny knees making a tent under the sheet, remembers her getting out of bed to use the shared chamber pot. He shores up these memories against her now. Something about the sight of the treetops brings back, like a strong stimulus rushing along his veins,

68

things he has put out of his mind—adventures with his gang of mates, yelling and fighting and running, crashing through brambles, pushing on until his heart beat as if it were bursting out of his chest. Now he mustn't move, with Ellen's head against him.

After a while Ellen sits up, relieved, and she and James have a cigarette. She finds it funny, the way he smokes nursing the cigarette with the tip in his palm, the end between his thumb and forefinger, drawing the smoke through his fist like the men on the docks. For once, James isn't afraid that Ellen thinks he's common. At this moment in the park, for some reason, the docks are something to impress her with—he doesn't even remind her that he's not one of those men, that he works in an office.

—You're smoking it down to the nub, he explains. —So's not to waste any, and so the foreman can't see.

Ellen tries it. It makes him laugh to see her bending her blonde head over the cigarette, coughing when the smoke goes up her nose. Then James pretends to smoke the way she does, taking quick puffs, waving the cigarette about with his little finger crooked. He wants to tell her all about himself, his future. He feels how he's fascinating to her—it's as if she's attached to him by some glistening thread which he can tug this way and that, and she'll turn her head with its coil of heavy hair to attend to whatever he shows her. He's aware of his own body slim and hard behind the dense cloth of his dark suit. It begins to fascinate him too, this power that belongs to his looks, to his nature. But just then Connie wakes up. There are bits of

69

leaf mould pressed into her cheek. She's groggy and bleary. She lies looking up at them balefully, as if she'd caught them out. Her mouth is twisted into an expression like a disgusted cat's. Her teeth are blue from the wine.

He can't talk properly to Ellen while Connie's looking.

*   *   *

He's glad afterwards he didn't talk about his father. He could have made a fool of himself: his brother Arthur says that Pa got the story out of a book. Connie probably thinks that too. But James has loved the story since he was a little boy. His pa was missing at sea before the war, and when he came back he said he'd been captured by natives in Madagascar, and that they'd made a god of him, dressing him in animal skins and drumming and dancing round him, sacrificing to him. When he escaped he got away with only a monkey and a pocket full of precious stones—their mother has a ruby made into a ring, with a claw setting. His story got into the papers with a photograph of him with the monkey (which he sold later) on his shoulder. James's mother still keeps the papers in a drawer, though after he came back Pa wasn't often in the house. She'd had to take in lodgers when they thought he was drowned, so there wasn't room. No one even told James till weeks afterwards that his father had died—of TB in the poor hospital—so he missed the funeral. Arthur and his mother and sisters knew about it; they didn't go because they didn't want to.

—Why would anyone make a god of him? says

70

Arthur with contempt.

—What about the rubies?

—It's not a ruby, it's a garnet. One garnet. I expect he won it cheating at cards. Or stole it.

Arthur's the clever one, apprenticed to a draughtsman. James keeps his mouth shut, he never wants to appear a fool in front of Arthur. But stubbornly he persists in believing that such transformations as happened to his father are possible somewhere. Once he's out of his apprenticeship, he'll present himself for examination at the Nellist Nautical School in Newcastle. He wants to become a master mariner, and have a ship of his own. (His timing's bad. By the time he does get his master's certificate, trade for the Merchant Navy will have slumped, and English rivers will be choked with tramp steamers requiring long-term berths.)

*　　　*　　　*

In the summer the girls go to Whitley Bay for a week, and James joins them there on his day off. He takes tea with them at the Park Hotel, where they have rooms, paid for by Mr Pearson; the ices are served in silver-plate dishes at a glass-topped table in the conservatory, while a trio plays music. Connie spoons hers up demurely, looking as though she's been doing this all her life. She uses the tongs to pick out sugar lumps for James, as if he were a kid on holiday, until he tells her to leave off. Afterwards they all go up to Ellen's room because Ellen wants to show James souvenirs of a couple of pals of hers who were killed in the war. The room is crowded and snug, with an armchair covered in pink silk, a

71

pink silk eiderdown, fringed lampshades. Ellen brings out the pals' photographs and the postcards they wrote, blacked out with ink where they were censored. She even has a lock of hair from one of them, Bunny, which she keeps in a book of poetry he gave her. Ellen's eyes well up with tears—real tears, so that her nose gets red and her mouth twists into an ugly shape. She has had her hair cut now, and the new style doesn't suit her heavy head the way it suits Connie's.

James pretends to be angry that he was too young to fight and do his bit, but really the faces in those photographs are too quenched and completed, he's tired of them. Arthur tried to enlist but they turned him down because of his varicose veins. Two of Connie's brothers were with the Tyneside Irish at the Somme, but she never cared for them much, she only wrinkles her nose when Ellen kindly tries to include them in her sorrowing. Anyway, they both came back, and they've been boozing and fighting their way round the docks ever since.

—Let's go for a swim, Connie says. —Let's walk down in our swimsuits.

—You can't do that, says James.

—We've done it every day. No one cares.

—It *is* Sunday, says Ellen warily.

The idea of the two of them flaunting themselves in the public street fills James with a boiling rage that somehow has to do with the dead soldiers. He thinks Connie is unpatriotic, shameless.

—I wouldn't allow any wife of mine to go parading round with nothing on in front of everybody, he says hotly.

Connie is delighted. —'Allow', Jimmy Mac? You

won't 'allow' it? Who d'you think you are, King of the Hottentots or something?

The weather's changing anyway, and Ellen decides it's too chilly for the swimsuits. They go and walk on the front and have their photograph taken sitting on an upturned boat, then struggle across the pebbles in the sea wind, the girls clinging to James, Ellen's beret blowing away and bowling off down the beach, James running like mad after it. He feels excitedly that they're all on the brink of something new, an entirely new way of living, apart from their parents. Anything could happen. They're all three laughing, Ellen too; she has forgotten to be mournful and dreamy, in spite of her dead friends. When he snatches up her beret she comes running after him, full tilt into him, almost knocking him over, so that he has to catch her to save her from falling. For a moment they're staggering together, she's warm in his arms—thanking him in breathless, gasping sentences, admiring how fast he runs. He doesn't let go. He kisses her beside her ear, a sort of kiss, though he hasn't kissed anyone since he was a baby. He can smell whatever it is that she puts on her hair. Over her shoulder he can see Connie pretending not to see them, crouching down to poke at something she's found among the pebbles.

To his surprise, in the evening Connie comes back with him on the train to Newcastle. She says she has to visit her dad, who isn't well. ('Stomach,' she says shortly when he asks what's wrong.) The two of them mostly sit in silence. Their mood is flat, the sea air has taken it out of them. Without Ellen, they're returned to all the ordinary things they know of one another. When Connie closes her eyes, the purplish-red lids seem unnaturally large below her neat definite eyebrows; her face is more naked than when her eyes are open and vigilant. She asks about his work at the boatyard and he makes it sound more important than it is. He says he's responsible for ordering the timbers and fittings, whereas in reality he's just answering the telephone and running errands.

—Ellen likes you, Connie says. —You could get a job with her dad's firm.

James frowns suspiciously, but he doesn't think she's teasing. He reminds her that he's going away.

—Oh, you and your old running away to sea. I don't know why your heart's so set on getting yourself drowned.

It's true that James was taken aback by the sight of the churning, pounding sea on the beach this afternoon, as if he'd somehow left it out of his calculations. He sees the sea in the docks every day but that's different—still and filthy.

—I won't drown, he says sturdily. —I'm lucky.

—Ellen's a nice girl. You could have a good life here.

But he's only just seventeen, it's too soon for him to be thinking of getting wed. Girls are always wanting to talk about weddings. There's no one else in their compartment; the little train dawdles through the evening rain. —Look what I found on the beach, Connie says, fishing in the purse she carries. —Close your eyes. Open your hand.

She used to give him sweets like this when they were children.

He closes his fingers around it. It's nothing much—just a bit of sea-washed glass, smooth to the touch, a frosted blue. She tells him to keep it safe

74

when he goes away, says it's her luck added on to his.

*   *   *

The *Trojan Prince*, carrying a general cargo of manufactured goods and foodstuffs, goes aground on rocks off the west coast of Canada, one evening of storm and fog in February 1923. Two men row heroically to shore, running a line from the davits of the trapped lifeboat, making it fast around a tree when they reach land. One by one the crew crosses to safety, the Captain last, hand over hand along the rope. Clinging on to that rope, sometimes the men are dangling fifteen feet above the waves; sometimes they're plunged fifteen feet deep beneath. The wind screams. Black walls of water pick up a ghostly illumination from the swirling snowflakes.

When it's his turn, apprentice James McIlvanney can't get rid of the idea that everything is happening in a story, to someone else whose role he seems to be carrying off convincingly. To his relief it turns out that this someone is not a coward: he's resourceful and determined and strong enough. Here he is, swinging above the terrible sucking water, above his certain death if he falls in. There's a rhythm to it—if you let the rhythm take you, then you know how to let go of the soaking slippery rope with one hand, twisting and lunging your body forward in mid-air, then clapping your hand on the rope again, farther along. He learned this when he was a boy climbing trees with his mates. He's hanging on for dear life. There ought to be somebody to see it. Then he's plunged under the water and his lungs are bursting. He loses his left

75

plimsoll in the crossing, also the bit of blue glass Connie Chappell gave him.

Somehow they all hang on. It's a wonder that there is no loss of life among the forty-two crewmen. But the ship can't be saved: it breaks up on the rocks over the next few days while they wait for rescue. Where they have got ashore is an uninhabited outcrop west of Vancouver Island, covered in scrub and stunted trees. They make a fire, and boil hot water to drink by melting the snow. The wireless operator didn't manage to signal their position before the wreck, and they can't find anywhere now to launch a distress rocket. The next day, when the storm subsides, the men go back on board to rescue what supplies and foodstuffs they can—mostly canned fruit. James finds a spare black boot, among the clothes they bring. Some of the men break into the bonded store, to get at the spirits.

The Captain sits apart from the rest of them, inconsolable at the loss of his ship. No one takes any notice of the four apprentice boys. James has time to think about the enormity of the task he has undertaken: acquiring the necessary knowledge to navigate the ocean using the stars. He makes up his mind to draft a table of all the subjects he needs to know, setting out the period of time he will dedicate to each. He resolves to adhere to this timetable even while he's in port, instead of going ashore with his shipmates.

James imagines telling all this to Connie when he gets home.

He's sorry that he lost the little token she gave him, which he kept in his pocket through all the first hard months of his apprenticeship at

Dartmouth, but it doesn't matter. She won't care, it was only a bit of glass.

On the third day they're spotted by Japanese fishermen, who alert the Bamfield lifeboat. Then they're taken by cutter to Seattle, and after that across Canada by train to St John in New Brunswick. From St John, James sends a postcard to Connie, telling her that he's all right. On board the Royal Mail steamer that takes them home, the officers and apprentices travel first class; the shipwreck has made them famous. Lady Furness, a patron of the Royal National Lifeboat Institution, helps James read the menu, which is written in French, and organises the apprentices in a tableau—'Survivors'—to entertain the other passengers. They sing 'Eternal Father Strong to Save'.

When they dock at Liverpool, Connie is waiting for him.

He knows he ought to marry Ellen Pearson and get a house full of furniture.

But he can't. He won't.

Because the Night

Their parents had fantastic parties, they were famous for it. The bath in the downstairs bathroom would be filled with ice, and then with bottles of Veuve du Vernay. All this was paid for on their father's entertainment account at the import–export company where he was managing director, and a lot of the guests would have to be dull Anglia World people to make this all right. But the Anglia World people didn't stay that long, and when they'd gone the party atmosphere changed, it was taken over by their parents' real friends, the ones they still had from university, or the ones their mother, Peggy, had met as a teacher and a painter.

When they were little Tom and Kristen were allowed to stay up late and run around, although it wasn't the sort of party where anyone else's children were invited. The au pair was meant to put them to bed but often the au pair—Annegret then Sylvie then Bengta—would be partying too: Annegret drooping her head shyly, tipping the drink from side to side in her wine glass, being chatted up by some teacher from Mum's school, Bengta dancing barefoot by herself, to Blondie or David Bowie or the Eurythmics. If it was summer there would be coloured flares burning among the flowers in the beds, grown-ups swinging in the dark in the two hammocks slung between the trees.

Tom was always good at inventing games, but the ones he made up on party nights were wilder. The children withdrew from the lit-up house; afloat in the dark, swollen with music and voices, it was hardly recognisable as the ordinary space they knew in daytime. Their house was on a hill at the edge of one of those minor towns in Surrey that are clustered up against the skirts of London; once it must have been in the countryside, but newer houses had been built around it, and pieces had been chopped off from their garden to go with each new one. But still they had a lawn with flower beds, and some huge old trees, and beyond that a tiny wood, about a third of an acre. At the back of this wood—reached by an earth path which wound past the tank with the oil for the central heating and the outhouse where the bikes and the lawnmower were kept—there were a couple of old greenhouses not used for anything. The children weren't supposed to play in these because of the broken glass, and because in one of them there was a deep well with a square stone across the top. But on party nights the greenhouses became their base.

Kristen wore the gauzy frilly Ossie Clark her mother had been married in, pulled up above her Brownie belt so she didn't trip on it; Tom would be in his soldier suit, red jacket unbuttoned, his pistol in its holster slung low on his hip. Their gym daps gave them extra silence and speed. Kneeling among the baked-dry leaves on the stone floor of the greenhouse with the well, they made plans. If the weather had been fine, the glass panes would hold in their pocket of heat long into the evening, pungent with the green smell of tomato stalks, even though no tomatoes ever grew in there any more, only fleshy tall weeds that spurted up wherever the rain leaked in, then died and parched to ghosts in the dry spells. The greenhouses were built of brick to about waist height; an aisle ran between raised beds of dry earth and shelves of empty flowerpots.

Kristen was assigned the easier tasks for their raids on the party, filling their water bottle at the tap in the kitchen, stealing food from where the buffet was laid out. Tom would try to put something alcoholic into his Action Man flask without being spotted. The grown-ups were their enemies, or at best neutral. As well as food and drink they took trophies: their mother's silver watch, left by the kitchen sink when Peggy washed her hands after putting out the party food; the keys to the Audi. Tom outrageously once even took a picture from the wall—not one of Peggy's, but an ink drawing by a man friend of hers, of a woman's ugly naked bosoms all by themselves, not attached to any other part of a body. The children hadn't known how they hated it until Tom lifted it coolly from its place in the hall and put it in his rucksack. They always put all the trophies back, next morning.

In these games Kristen worked herself up into a fever of resentment against the grown-ups, which she never felt the rest of the time. Ordinarily she was passionately attached to her family, also to Annegret and Sylvie and Bengta in turn (and for ever, after they left); she was homesick whenever she was parted from them. At the parties, her feeling of alienation from them all was like a hunger in her chest: whatever she and Tom took wasn't enough, couldn't fill this greedy, aching, thrilling space.

*   *   *

That was when they were little. Tom didn't want anything to do with the parties any more, he made a retching noise at the idea of their parents and

80

their parents' friends dancing and messing around in hammocks. When a party was planned the summer he was sixteen, he arranged to be out all night, staying with boys from school. Lots of things had changed since the old days. They didn't have au pairs any more. On Sylvie's last morning, when Jim had to drive her to the airport very early, she had left a message beside Kristen's pillow, written in lipstick on a tissue; Kristen unfolded it and gazed at it every night before she went to sleep, breathing its perfume, until the tissue dissolved into pink dust.

Now Kristen let herself in at the front door every school afternoon with the key which she wore around her neck on a string. Stirring up the empty air in the hall, she was alert to the secret breathing of the house, the boiler clicking and creaking as the heating came on, the tiny thudding of the cat stepping downstairs. Kristen didn't hate her girls' independent school; she had plenty of friends and did reasonably well in most subjects. But when she shut the door behind her it was such a relief to be alone, away from the jostle of green uniforms— dropping her briefcase, pushing off her outdoor shoes without undoing the laces, then standing in her socks in the kitchen (which the cleaner would have tidied), making strawberry milkshake and toast with peanut butter. Watching children's TV, sitting among the big floor cushions in the glass extension room, she seeped back gradually into her real self. The knowledge that her mother would be home in an hour (Dad picked up Tom and they came later) was a cocoon, keeping her safe, yet also apart and immune.

As long as the Pune wasn't around.

Sometimes when Kristen thought she was all

81

alone in the house, she'd suddenly hear him moving about upstairs, or using the lavatory (which he didn't bother to flush), or running water into the kettle in the kitchen. He didn't speak to her—even if sometimes he came in and sat watching television with her—but his being there spoiled everything. He was supposed to live with his own mother half a mile away on one of the new estates (ghastly but expensive, Peggy said), though he was twenty-one, old enough to have left home long ago. But he moaned on to Peggy about his mother, he claimed she was driving him mad, he followed Peggy around going over word by word whatever latest awful thing his mother had said, which Peggy analysed with the special air of patient, amused exasperation that she reserved for him. His dad was dead, or had left home, or something.

Peggy said to the Pune that there was always a room for him in their house, by which she meant the room which used to belong to the au pairs; he said their house was the only place he could express what he really felt. And so he began to use this room as his own whenever he stayed, filling it with cigarette smoke, and cassette tapes, and bottles of the pills he had to take, and dirty clothes he never sorted out for washing (the cleaner wouldn't go in there). He never opened the curtains, he slept in late: Kristen guessed that often he only got out of bed when she came back in the afternoon after a whole day of travelling and lessons and playtimes and school dinner. Tom started calling this room the Pune-hole.

Peggy had taught the Pune when he was still at school. She wasn't the ordinary kind of teacher, she worked with the kids who needed special help, which usually meant very thick or very naughty, but sometimes meant weirdos like the Pune (whose real name was Simon), clever but out of their mind. She had helped him through his A levels and then to get into Sussex University, where he had lasted one year before coming back to live with his mother again.

—It's funny how although he hates his mother so much he can't get away from her, their dad said.

—Well of course, darling. That's the whole point.

The Pune only loved their house when Peggy was in it. Alone there with Jim or Tom or Kristen, he was crucified if they spoke to him. Mostly, until Peggy was home, he skulked in his room, only venturing out to refill his mug with the horrible coffee he made, three heaped teaspoons of granules, no milk or sugar. He was tall and skinny, with bad posture and glasses with thick black rims; he pushed back the greasy hair flopping in his face with a twitching movement, so that the naked long cheekbones and jaw-line beneath were visible in flashes. When he sat with Kristen in the afternoons he reacted to the TV programmes as if she wasn't there: groaning, dropping his head in his hands, giving off shouts of derision like gunshots. He used their ornaments for ashtrays.

When Peggy came in, hallooing at the front door with her ringing, singing voice, the Pune would home in on her straight away, like some needy kind of pet. (They'd had a grown-up cat like this once, who meowed without stopping and sucked Tom's sleeves.) Peggy would make a point of coming in to kiss Kristen, asking how her day had been at school, how she'd done in her French test.

—All right, said Kristen, altering the position of her head around the kiss so as not to lose sight for a

83

moment of the television screen. —Not too bad.

—I have to talk to you, the Pune said to Peggy.
—I've had this incredible dream. You were in it,
of course. We were at the zoo together, you and
me. We looked through the bars of all the cages at
the animals, and they were looking back at us, only
not with animal expressions, it was as if they knew
everything about us, better than we did. I was afraid
of them, I wanted to go, but then it turned out that
you, only you, could communicate with them.

—Like Doctor Dolittle, Kristen suggested.

He was annoyed. —Well, no, not like Doctor
Dolittle.

—Just give me a minute, Simon. Give me time to
draw breath.

You could hear Peggy was fed up with him, but
at the same time she couldn't help wanting to find
out what he'd been dreaming about her. Kristen
got to know a certain expression on her mother's
face, whenever the Pune was with her: guarded and
curious, with a spot of feverishness in her cheeks.
Peggy was small and compact with pale skin and big
eyes with thin, sensitive lids; she had a mass of red
hair, just beginning to be threaded with grey, which
was always a statement however she wore it: loose,
or pinned up with ribbons, or in a swinging plait.
Kristen was small and pale like her mother but her
hair was nondescript. Peggy dressed brilliantly too,
in green dungarees and striped satin shirts and old
flowered party dresses from junk shops: this was
one of the things that made her stand out from
the company wives at the parties (by this time Jim
had moved on from Anglia World to Transglobal
Services).

If Kristen went into the kitchen when children's

84

programmes had finished, the Pune would be sitting at the table still holding forth, while Peggy in her apron was getting supper ready. By this time he would have lapsed from his excitement at the beginning of the conversation, and sunk into despair about himself. This was their pattern, familiar as a ball game: he chucked the unravelling bundles of his despair, Peggy fielded them and beamed back her resilient brightness.

—I can't talk to girls; I don't know what they want to talk about. They run a mile when they see me coming. I'll be the only twenty-one-year-old virgin left on the planet.

—Don't be silly, Simon. Peggy would be batting out escalopes of pork with her rolling pin and flouring them. —You're an exceptionally attractive young man, with your gorgeous looks and your brains. The only thing you haven't got is belief in yourself.

—They'll want to talk to me about their feelings, he said gloomily. —I don't know about anybody else's feelings.

The Pune had the sense not to want to discuss this subject around Jim and Tom; when they came in he'd stare fixedly into his empty mug, wrapping his long legs together under the table. He was shy of anyone seeing his face, but Kristen was always having to notice the gap between his sagging loon trousers and half-unbuttoned grubby shirt: the stretch of lean belly was whorled with surprisingly vigorous black hair, heading in a bristling line down into the fraying waistband of his underpants. He wore his socks without shoes around the house, which Kristen wasn't supposed to do. It disturbed Kristen, when she and the Pune sat watching TV

85

side by side with their legs stretched out, to know that they had even this one accidental detail in common; though hers were tidy fawn regulation socks, and his would very likely not even be a pair, and often had a white knobbly potato-toe poking out from a hole in one of them.

—He's a bit of a poor specimen, Jim said, —you must admit.

—He's actually a very good-looking boy, said Peggy, —if you look below the surface of his problems.

—He's so puny, said Tom (this was where the nickname came from). —His wrists are so skinny, they look like they'd break if they had to hold up more than a cup of coffee; and he can't even hold that, he spills everything. He's always staggering about, falling over his own feet.

Red-headed Tom was small and hard and solid, invaluable in the rugby first fifteen at Dulwich College.

Jim said he was blinded by the surface and couldn't get past it.

*   *   *

Kristen didn't know how to dress up for this party. She messed around for hours in her bedroom, putting things on then taking them off again: she was too old for stuff from the play box, not old enough to look right in grown-up clothes. Her new breasts, little pyramids of fat, embarrassed her whatever she wore. In the end she resorted to an inconspicuous pull-on denim skirt and T-shirt, devoting herself to decorating her head instead, screwing her hair up in joke knots and plaiting in bits of beading and lace, glueing sequins above her eyes. She could have had a friend over, Peggy had offered it; she had dithered over who she should ask, then with relief abandoned the idea. She got on well with everyone in her crowd at school, but whenever she brought any of them home she suffered from a strange dissociation the whole time, as if this wasn't her *real* home but another parallel place resembling it in every detail.

Before he cycled off to his friend's house, Tom came into her room with instructions. His eyebrows—faint dark brush strokes, not red—lifted in surprise at the sight of her hair decor, but it would have been beneath his dignity to comment.

—Keep an eye on the Pune, Kristie. Don't let him make an idiot of himself. I'd stick pretty close to Mum, in case he starts shooting his mouth off to her in front of all her friends.

These days all his campaigns were directed against one thing: the Punic Wars, he called them. Kristen had no intention of spending her evening standing guard over her mother. Before the party began she stowed supplies among the flowerpots in the greenhouse: two slices of Peggy's lemon fridge cake in a Tupperware box, apples, and the old Action Man flask filled up with sherry. Sherry wasn't really what anyone drank at parties, but it was the only alcoholic drink she liked, so far. She also put a candle and a box of matches ready, and for a few minutes felt excited, then silly, because nothing could really happen if she was all by herself. But the greenhouse might be a good place to hide away in, if the party was awful.

The sky was shut under a grey lid of cloud, the late afternoon was limply warm. Kristen ran a bath for her mother, combining scented oils like a witch mixing potions; once she thought she heard, behind the thunder of the tap, waves of rain insisting at the open windows, but when she looked out the garden was still dry and blank. Her dad was hanging paper lanterns in the trees. Peggy's 1950s strapless evening dress, green silk, was laid out on the bed with her new strapless bra, new tights still in their packet, ropes of beads; in a glass on the dressing table was the yellow rose she'd cut in the garden for her hair. When Peggy had finished setting out the food the caterers had delivered, she came upstairs to change.

—That bath smells extraordinary. I suppose it's safe to get in, I won't turn into a frog or anything?

Undressing, she scrutinised her daughter in rapid assessment. —What are you going to wear, darling?

—This, said Kristen briefly. She looked away from the sight of her mother in her underwear, the complicated adult voluptuousness. —D'you like my sequins?

Peggy baulked for one audible instant then forgave her. —You're rather wonderful, she said. —You're like . . .

—No, shut up, don't say what I'm like.

*　　　*　　　*

The Pune, miraculously, wasn't the first to arrive, as Tom had predicted he would be. And when he did come he looked quite like a normal human being, he'd changed out of the usual Pune-wear into a black polo-neck top with black trousers. He walked round everywhere with his cigarette in his hand, of course, sucking on it as if it was the first one he'd had in weeks; and his trousers were too short, they showed stretches of hairy leg when he sat on the

88

floor with his knees up in front of him. He wasn't any good at the polite stuff like talking to strangers, but some of the teachers from school knew him and got down on the floor with him, even when the party was really still in its stage for standing up chatting, holding on to plates and glasses. The group on the floor seemed to have more fun, they were shrieking with laughter. Kristen was sure she heard him telling them the thing about him being the only twenty-one-year-old virgin left.

Kristen moved around between the clusters of guests for a while, standing at the edge of each one with her glass of juice, looking from face to face as they spoke, responding politely if they made an effort to include her. But there wasn't much they could ask her about, apart from school: she saw herself insignificant, as if from a great distance, her inner life compacted into a small flat tasteless cake. She got tired of telling them that chemistry was her favourite subject; they seemed to think this meant she would go on to win a Nobel Prize or something, though she didn't really like it all that much, she just found the chemistry lab an orderly and tranquillising place. Peggy kissed Kristen and squeezed her tight against the green dress: its skirts stood out stiffly, the material crackled and was scratchy like coarse paper. —My daughter is the most sensible girl in the world, she said. —Much more sensible than her mother. Don't be fooled by the crazy plaits.

A Transglobal wife said Peggy was so clever to wear something old, she'd never dare. Kristen slipped away to watch television in her bedroom, but the waves of noise from below made it difficult to concentrate. After a while departing guests, looking for the room where they'd left their coats, came trekking past her door, and sometimes even opened it by mistake and peered inside: it must be odd for them to stumble on this pocket of dullness tucked away inside the noisy adventure of the party. The music was beginning to get louder: 'Dancing in the Street', then 'Relax, Don't Do It', then 'Purple Rain'. She went to see if things had taken off at last, half sliding on her bottom down the banister; her dad was crossing the hall, fetching more wine from the downstairs bathroom. In photographs from when he was young Jim was almost unrecognisable, with bare feet and long hair; that wild past self was packed away inside his genial, paunchy, present one, and his hair now was normal, wearing thin at the temples and on top. Jim could answer all the difficult questions on the quiz programmes; he seemed too solidly knowledgeable ever to have been a hippie.

—What are you up to, Pigeon? Are you having a nice time?

—I hate parties.

—Oh God, he said, exaggeratedly glumly. —So do I.

With his shirtsleeves rolled up and his tie loosened, hands bristling with bottles, he didn't look as if he wasn't enjoying himself; the tie would come off altogether, later. —I suppose you're pretty snug in your little bolt-hole of a bedroom. Are you foraging for food?

—You can come and watch telly with me if you like.

—Don't tempt me. I'm a slave chained to the wheel of pleasure down here.

She stepped out through the door in the extension room, into the garden. Coloured paper lanterns were strung across the patio, floating like balloons filled weightlessly with light; the night stood back among surprised pale trees, cigarette smoke hung motionless. Peggy had put out a rug on the flagstones, and all the big floor cushions: she was sitting cross-legged in a circle of friends like an audience, the Pune lying stretched out with his head in her lap. If Kristen could slip behind the trellis which screened the oil tank, then she could make her escape to the greenhouses.

—What do you know about our life? Peggy was saying to the Pune, in an amused, scratchy, drawling voice that made Kristen think of the surface of the green dress. Peggy never got really drunk, but if other people were drinking she arrived at a state like an exaggerated performance of her usual self: she held court, she was opinionated and funny, she was less tolerant.

—Are you accusing us?

All the time she was doing something to the Pune's hair. He had his eyes closed. He had taken his glasses off and was holding them in his hand; she was pushing back the long fringe from his white forehead, raking through it with her fingernails (which she had had painted crimson for the party). The sight of his naked head embarrassed Kristen, reminding her of swimming lessons at school, familiar friends translated into seal-creatures under sleeked wet hair, all ears and eyes.

—I know about Transglobal Services, for instance, said the Pune.

—Who's that? asked somebody.

Jim had arrived in the open doorway. —They paid for the wine, he said. —So don't bite the bloody hand.

The Pune craned his head for a moment up off

91

Peggy's lap, blinking in Jim's direction. —The bloody hand, he said, —it's just that. Don't enquire too closely into where the money comes from, for this lovely house on the hill.

He was trying to pick one of his fights over politics: about some company Jim said was only a TGS subsidiary anyway.

—Nobody's allowed to spoil my party mood, said Jim. —Don't even let him get started.

Peggy was drawing out long strands of the Pune's hair, tugging at them. —What about me? she said, in a fake-pleading voice. —Don't I do good? Haven't I done good to you, ungrateful boy?

—As I'm sure you're aware, Jim went on, —European Community sanctions prohibit the export of any military hardware to South Africa.

—But you export them to an Italian firm, which sells them on.

—Don't be simple-minded. It's not the manufacturers who make the wars.

—That's debatable, said one of Peggy's friends from school.

—Decent jobs and economic stability are more use to them than your pure fucking thoughts.

—I don't have any pure thoughts, said the Pune. —Only fucking ones.

Peggy started pushing at him, to roll him off her lap. —Go away, you're being horrid. I don't like you very much tonight.

—You sound just like my mother.

—I'm beginning to sympathise with your mother.

* * *

Kristen stepped backwards out of the light, into

92

the shadow of the oil tank: no one saw her vanish. From her new perspective, the purple clematis flowers growing thick on the trellis loomed suddenly momentous against the party-glow; the grown-up talk dropped into blurred lively noise, as if she had crossed a frontier. On her side of it was the night-quiet, a bird blundering in the bushes, a dank breath of earth, a rattle when her skirt caught on the shiny laurel leaves. She hadn't brought out her torch; when she turned to follow the path back past the bike shed into the wood, the blackness at first was like a wall preventing her. After a few moments' staring, it melted into grey, seeped into by the light of the party behind. Imagining being blind, with her eyes strained open and her hands feeling out all round her, lifting her knees high in case she stumbled, she made her way cautiously past the shed and then on into the denser dark of the wood. Tom would have remembered the torch.

At one point she pitched forward over a root, then crawled for a few yards on her hands and knees, her own breathing sounding in her ears as if it was someone else's. Arriving at the back end of the greenhouse, she had to feel her way round to the front through clumps of nettles; the door when she pulled it open screamed like an animal. At the end of all these trials, it seemed against the odds that the candle would really be where she had left it, or that she would have thought to bring matches; but she put her hands on both of them easily.

The flare of light was a miracle. Careless of hot wax, she planted the lit candle in a pot of crumbled earth; the flame reflected liquidly on glass panes, enclosing her in the blackness outside. Her hands and knees were muddy and the skin on her legs was coming up in red welts from the nettles. She sat on the tiled floor in a thin layer of chill rising from the earth beneath, distinct from the held-in day's warmth under the glass; warily she swallowed a mouthful of the sherry, then ate one slice of lemon fridge cake, although she had eaten some already, in her bedroom. She felt herself going through the motions of the adventures a child might have—in an artificial, nostalgic way, because she wasn't really a child any more. You couldn't be, once you were thinking about what you were doing as childish.

Once, she and Tom had pushed aside the heavy lid of the well and dropped stones into it, to see if it was deep: it was deep enough to fall into, but there hadn't been any water in it, only a blind disappointing bottom of debris whose colour had decayed to rotten brown. The effects of the sherry began to flood through her; she swallowed more mouthfuls, tasting through the sweetness the plastic lip of the toy flask. When she became aware of the noise of someone approaching through the wood, it took her a few moments to feel properly afraid: at first she thought it might be Tom, back from his friends' house, but the sounds were too indefinite, too blundering. It could be anyone, any stranger or madman. Guiltily she shrank: she shouldn't be out here alone, burning a candle.

Someone called out for her. —Kristie?

It wasn't her father either.

She waited, to be sure, for the Pune's shape to detach itself from the surrounding darkness and lurch into view in the greenhouse doorway. —It had to be you, he said. —I saw a light shining through the trees. I was drowning, wandering round in the dark out there.

The greenhouse was invaded by his awkward height and limbs; she felt an outraged pang for her lost loneliness. He dropped to sit cross-legged opposite her in the narrow space. —It stinks of booze in here. What are you drinking?

—Sherry.

—Extraordinary. Is there any left?

Silently she handed him the flask. He drank from it, wiped the top, then handed it back as if for her turn; she was almost indignant that he didn't query whether it was sensible for her to be drinking, at her age. After a moment's hesitation she swigged deeply.

—This is nice, he said. —I never noticed there was a greenhouse before.

He got out his Golden Virginia tobacco tin and began rolling up by candlelight, not an ordinary cigarette but one of the druggy ones Tom specially resented, with something sprinkled in it out of a little bag. (—Our parents could be arrested, you know, Tom said, —for allowing this to go on under their roof.) The drink's strong effect coiled powerfully in Kristen, pushing out of her mouth in words a thought she hardly knew she'd had.

—I suppose you and my mum are having a lovers' tiff.

He flicked his lighter and sucked in his cheeks, shaking back his hair, drawing flame into his raggedy cigarette; after the first deep pull into his lungs, he turned it round in his fingers to admire it. —We're not actually lovers, he said in a strangulated voice, holding the smoke in. —Not in the sense of sexual consummation. I don't think she'd ever really let me near her. Anyway I never dared try, in case she turned me down. D'you want some?

He held out the cigarette to Kristen.

—No thank you, she said, her cheeks burning primly.

—But I suppose we have had a tiff. I'm in a mess over your mother. I can't seem to cope unless I've got her around, and I'm terrified she'll take herself away. Then I say precisely the things that make her most angry.

Kristen seemed to be in a moon-terrain where naked facts lay around for anyone to find.

—So why not just take yourself away instead?

He didn't notice she was being rude. —Don't imagine I haven't thought of that. But I'm weak, pathetically weak. He closed his eyes and yawned, leaning his head back against the brick ledge. —I could be happy, in a place like this. It's nice in here.

—There's a well, you know.

—A real well?

—But no water in it. Tom and I looked.

—You didn't bring out any food?

Kristen gave the Pune the second slice of lemon fridge cake, she ate an apple down to its stalk, they finished the sherry. He described some film he'd seen, where angels came to earth, and one of them fell in love with an acrobat and took on mortal form to be with her. He was just the same as when he was an angel, except that there was a bald patch in his hair and his clothes didn't suit him. —But it was all worth it, the Pune said. —In exchange for mortal love. So the film said. What do you think?

(Tom said afterwards that he'd heard of this film, and it was pretentious crap.)

—I don't know, said Kristen.

He yawned again. —Go and tell Peggy I'm out

96

here. Tell her I need her, tell her I'm in a state, tell her I'm going to do something desperate.

—I'll have to take the candle, she warned him.

*   *   *

Walking back to the party, she held up her curved hand to shield the candle flame from the draught of her movement. She did deliver the Pune's message, but not to Peggy.

—Simon's in the greenhouse, she said to Jim when she met him.

He was piling up his plate from the wrecked remains of the buffet set out on the dining table. In the front room Peggy was dancing to 'Because the Night' (her favourite), with the artist who'd drawn the bosoms Kristen and Tom had stolen years ago.

—Simon? What greenhouse? You mean our old greenhouse?

—He wants Mum to go out to him. He says he needs her.

—He can go fuck himself, said Jim. —Excuse my French, Pigeon.

—Are you going to tell her?

—No, I don't think I am.

Then Kristen went upstairs to her bedroom, and changed into her pyjamas. All the time she was nursing her drunkenness as tenderly as if it was the candle flame, carrying herself upright, planting one foot in front of another, choosing small sensible words that she could hold like little stones in her mouth. She used the bathroom, stood up and was slightly sick into the toilet, washed her hands and cleaned her teeth, stretched back her lips and bared her teeth at her image in the cabinet mirror.

97

Switching off the light in her bedroom, she stood at the window looking out; one of the paper lanterns in the trees had caught fire and was blazing up, the flare illuminating a pale mass of leaves shocked out of night-time invisibility. She had left Simon by himself, out in the greenhouse in the dark: it was a triumph in their Punic Wars.

*   *   *

And then she was leaping and pounding back across the grass and into the wood, mounds of breasts bouncing under her pyjamas, hardly noticing the sharp sticks and rocks that cut at her bare feet.

The Pune couldn't really have thrown himself in the well. A child might just about fall into it, but it wasn't wide enough for an adult, they would only get stuck if they tried: she pictured his feet sticking up out of the well and waving around, a sob of breathy derision ripped her chest. Anyway, it hadn't been all that far down to the dry bottom when she and Tom had looked, only ten feet or so, perhaps not that much. The torch beam—she had remembered, this time, to snatch the torch from Tom's room on her way out—jagged and bobbed in front of her as she ran, breath hiccuping in her ears; she trained it at the rough ground ahead, leaping over roots and dodging past the old wheelbarrow tipped on its side, a broken go-kart.

But there were other ways to die. Some awful tearing heaving noise came from the dark greenhouse as the torch beam found it, catching first on the rusting ornate pinnacle of the gable above the door, then reflecting off filthy panes overgrown with ivy. The iron frame shook. Through the glass, quenching

98

her in horror, Kristen seemed to see a black shape hanging; then at the shape's centre suddenly, as if a spirit struggled out, a small light bloomed and spurted.

Kristen had forgotten that the Pune had his lighter.

She stepped into the doorway.

—Hello, he said. —Don't tell me. She wouldn't come.

—I didn't say anything to her. She was busy dancing.

—Don't worry. She wouldn't have come anyway.

—Are you OK?

—You were wrong. Look: there is water in it.

She should have recognised the noise she heard: he had been heaving aside the great stone that covered the entrance to the well, more easily than she and Tom had moved it, both pushing together. He was holding up his lighter over the opening; she tilted down her torch beam. Light slid on slick black, nearer to the top than she was expecting.

—But it really was dry, when we looked.

—It'll be a spring. They can dry up in a drought and then come back again. Find something to throw down.

Kristen remembered seaside pebbles, lined up along the windowsill; when they dropped them in, one at a time, the well swallowed them with an intimate small wet gulp, an old sound not given out for years. The Pune stared after them. His face was washed in the light shining back from the well's surface: the long slanting lines of his cheekbones, the pits of his eye-hollows, the gathered concentration.

He and Kristen exchanged smiles of satisfaction.

Journey Home

His sister changed her relationship status on Facebook to single. Alec didn't do Facebook, but he checked on hers fairly often, because there were only the two of them, no one else to look out for her (one parent dead and one a mess). It probably meant nothing; she was always falling out with this latest boyfriend. Alec thought the boyfriend was no good. He texted Emmie anyway.

All that morning, his faint consciousness of worry floated against the greenish Venice light. He was staying in a residential centre, a modern block attached to a monastery on San Giorgio; it had been raining for days, he had to dry his wet clothes by hanging them along the lukewarm radiators in his room. Tourists in gondolas draped themselves under the blue tarpaulins, the front of St Mark's fumed, pavements were awash or greasy with salt spray; he had imagined that flood water must wash over out of the canals, but it seemed to seep out of the foundations of the buildings. The water in the Grand Canal flowed undulating and fast, glaucous green; the famous facades withdrew, forbidding, behind their winter veil of rain. As Alec hurried under his umbrella, his writing about the paintings sccmcd a heat source inside him like the blood reds of the paint, less mental than visceral.

He switched his phone off while he was working in the archives in the Frari, turned it on again when he came out—startled, after receding so far inside the study room's velvety quiet, at being buffeted again by the weather in the bustling, splashy, narrow *calle*.

100

The light smoked and was brownish, reflecting off the high walls in the rain. His Italian wasn't really good enough for deciphering the old documents; he was afraid he had wasted this morning, his last morning. And there was nothing on his phone from Em. Usually she was quick to get back to him; she spent too much time on her iPhone, hunkered angular on the floor in coloured thick tights and lace-up boots, presiding over the realm of her connections. Finely made, with narrow wrists and fingers, delicate ears, she was only twenty-two; when she was fifteen, she'd once taken an overdose of pills. She was pretty like a doll, with black hair cut in a short bob, and a strained, wide, eager smile. Alec had asked her what she saw in this latest guy. —Sex, she'd said, deliberately to embarrass him and shut him up. —Not everyone's an intellectual like you.

Alec was flying home next day; he wove through the crowds of umbrellas and slick waterproofs towards the Accademia, meaning to pay his farewell visit to Titian's *Pietà*, which was at the centre of his idea, and his book. But at the last minute he joined the press across the Rialto instead, went to his usual restaurant and ate risotto with peas and ham, drank a half-carafe of straw-coloured wine. The restaurant had all its lights on in the early afternoon, gloom had so thickened outside the windows; passers-by seemed to weave in an underground labyrinth. He could return to the Accademia after lunch: packing wouldn't take him half an hour; he had hardly colonised with his belongings his little cell, which despite its microwave and wireless connection was somehow appropriately monkish.

Its monkishness had suited him. He was beginning to think it might be his preference, his character, to be alone—with all the mixed package of banality and elevation that brought. It was banal, for instance, to be eating here by himself, calculating how many euros he had left, feeling the faint dampness of his clothes that had never thoroughly dried out. There was a mismatch between the Renaissance magnificence of his inner life and this flat surface on which magnificence scarcely showed up. The forms that were his imagination's language seemed untranslatable into a contemporary idiom. Alec had chosen art history, or it had chosen him, ten years ago, inter-railing in his gap year, finding his own way to the galleries that didn't interest his friends: the Magdalene running, arms upraised, out of the *Pietà* had seemed to bring some message for him.

Now he hesitated over returning to it for a last renewal. He didn't want the painting to fail to shock him—its depth and timbre and huge occupation of actual space, which could not be carried away in any mental picture, nor reproduced in copy. Over his espresso, then counting out euro notes on to the bill in its saucer, he hovered between obligations— not to miss the encounter, not to spoil it. The rain was falling now in earnest, blown against the walls in spasms like slaps from wet washing; the gallery would be full of sodden tourists with no interest in art. Perversely, that didn't make him head back to San Giorgio and a last session of endeavour on his laptop, or a few more hours, reading, wrapped up for warmth in his duvet.

He went straight through the galleries to the *Pietà*, not looking for once right or left at what tempted him from every wall, and found room on the bench in front of it. The murmuring, damp, texting, flirting teenagers crowding him in impersonal intimacy (one group Spanish, one American) hardly spared the painting's murky browns and blacks a second glance, but they weren't a distraction; in an emptier room his emotions might have been less concentrated. His friends (and Emmie) imagined that art was good for you, elevating and purifying like yoga or cutting down alcohol; they envied its virtue vaguely, and put off getting round to it. And his throb of recognition in front of the painting was pleasure: it was sensual, stronger than drink. But it wasn't consolation. In the archive he had been reading about how after Titian's death and the death of his son in the plague of 1576, the house where they had worked and lived like princes was ransacked in the general chaos, the paintings dispersed. The *Pietà* seemed to be news from such a world: the running Magdalene, Christ's body dead-white across his mother's lap, Jerome an old man naked and crawling. Worse is always possible past the worst thing you're afraid of.

*   *   *

He had to change at Paris for his flight to Aberdeen. It had been foggy in the early morning when they took off from Marco Polo, but there had been no warning of problems ahead. In Paris, however, it was snowing, and their onward flight had been postponed. Still he'd had no contact from Emmie. He texted her again, letting her know he was delayed. Then he texted Maggie, a mutual friend: 'Have you seen Em? Is she OK?' A bald, shallow snow-light reflected on to the airport's interior surfaces, equalising them so the spaces seemed dimensionless. Everyone was drawn to look out through the glass to where more snow was falling, so thickly that at times

103

you couldn't see through it; when it thinned, the shapes of planes loomed oversized, clumsily innocent in motionlessness. Nothing was taking off.

Alec had brought Gell's *Art and Agency* in his hand luggage and he tried to read it, but mostly it was impossible to concentrate. He was washed through with a succession of reactions—exasperation, resignation, panic. Maggie texted him that she had seen Em at the weekend with Aaron (the boyfriend), and that she had seemed fine. Alec could have asked Maggie to go round and check on her (Maggie knew about Em's history), but felt shame at this fussing over his sister, almost uxorious. He also felt fatalistic, an atom dropped arbitrarily in the vast stalled machinery of travel: what could he effect? It was half a relief. The airport wasn't quieter than usual, but he caught himself listening for what was missing—the perpetual machine-room hum of purposive forward motion, whose absence was scarcely perceptible and yet altered everything, tipping it into doubt.

He began to get to know the little group of his fellow passengers for Aberdeen. He and a couple of other men took turns to keep each other's places while they went scouting for information, and to stretch their legs. People were getting hungry; beyond where they had all come through security, there were only snack food outlets selling coffee and croissants. Then came news that their flight was cancelled; they had to queue for tickets on alternative flights, either to Aberdeen next day or to Edinburgh and Glasgow. The two young women assigned to oversee the process were thin and tired-looking, heavily made up. They did their best to placate the frustrated travellers, but their English was limited to a few stock phrases, and they were overruled by a man with a morose face like crumpled leather, who made a languid importance out of keeping all information to himself; in their blue uniforms, cut tight around the breasts and knees, they were somehow at his mercy.

A Romanian couple, too neat in their best clothes, travelling for the first time to visit their daughter, couldn't speak a word of French or English; Alec talked on their phone to the daughter in Aberdeen, she translated to her parents what he explained. In the mid-afternoon the snowfall stopped and the sky flaunted again, a surprising blue. There was activity outside, men with snowploughs conferring and gesticulating, and an impression of flights being called in far-flung other limbs of the airport. Then daylight was extinguished beyond the windows, and darkness changed the passengers' mood, bringing dread. A girl travelling home with her boyfriend began storming and sobbing, cursing. She was tall and heavy with sensible short hair and a stuffed toy pinned into one pocket of her rucksack. The resentment of the whole group seemed gathered up for a moment in her Scots righteousness, like a tight skin full to bursting.

The official would only respond in French, not looking directly at the flushed, plain girl but addressing the whole group, as if with a rage of disdain he'd been constrained to hold in until now. He had been patient and made efforts on their behalf; now their rudeness had changed everything, they would not be issued with tickets for any further flights. —No more tickets! he shouted suddenly in English. The passengers got the gist of it and responded in an opening scatter of indignant protest. Alec stood up and tried to negotiate with the man, doing his best in French. He explained that all they asked was to be kept informed and comfortable; they were hungry. At least the decent long coat he'd bought last winter gave him gravitas; no one could mistake him these days for a student. After a short wait, trays of sandwiches arrived with coffee and bottles of water. He found himself informally a bit of a hero in the little group; people asked for his opinion on the situation, or shared theirs with him.

No more flights left that night. It began to snow again. Mattresses were given out, so thin that Alec decided he was better off in his seat. Impulsively, late, he decided to ask Maggie after all to go round to check on Emmie; he stood by the window to make the call, where the stale light of the airport abutted on to blackness beyond. But Maggie didn't pick up—probably she'd already gone to bed. Alec touched his forehead against the cold of the glass. His phone was running out of battery, and the charger was packed in his suitcase.

*   *   *

All the next day they waited. In the morning it snowed; in the afternoon blue sky showed itself again and the snowploughs went out, but apparently to no effect. Tedium bulked substantial as a wall across the hours. From time to time a flare of anticipation roused, that flights were imminent—then sank again. As daylight faded, they were told they would be accommodated in hotels for this second night; they queued for coaches. Feeling drawn ever more deeply aside out of their real lives, they travelled for an hour in the dark, along roads deep in mysterious snow.

They were dropped in Disneyland, at a hotel like

a chateau cut out in plastic; in the foyer an inflatable Mickey Mouse strained upwards from where it was anchored, its rictus of merriment not reflected in the faces of the staff at the desk below. Along the identical empty corridors, oversized Snow Whites and Donald Ducks were set at intervals. It was a huge relief, to shower and be alone. Alec wondered what it meant, this exchange of his cell in Venice for another one, whose essential ingredients—warmth, bed, bathroom—were hardly different. Perhaps the existence of this non-place made the other one nothing too, and the paintings nothing. He lost his conviction that things could be themselves and not simply copies of other things, and was oppressed by a foggy anxiety, as if a catastrophe had happened somewhere offstage, beyond where he could reach to intervene in it. He tried to call Em again, from the handset beside the bed, but she didn't answer.

*   *   *

Next morning, after doughnuts and croissants in a half-timbered bar, the coach returned them to the airport; it was snowing again and their wait resumed. Then late that afternoon, with no advance warning or any obvious change in the weather, a flight to Aberdeen was called, and Alec got on it, along with most of those who'd waited with him. They were subduedly jubilant, doubting their luck until the very moment the plane was in the air. The journey only took an hour; at the Aberdeen end there was no fuss, they were used to snow. Needless to say, his suitcase with his clothes and his notes and several expensive books from the university library packed in it didn't arrive with him. He hadn't seriously expected it, and queued to fill out lost luggage forms.

He got the taxi to drop him off at Em's place. It wasn't actually snowing but it was a shock after the sealed atmosphere of the airport to find himself out alone in the deep mess of trodden snow and the raw cold. He didn't have the right shoes on, nor scarf and gloves. Em lived in a housing association flat in Rosemount behind Union Street; she didn't answer the door, and when he picked his way round to the back of the block he saw there were no lights on. He supposed he had better go home; he should have kept his taxi—he lived in the old university town, too far to walk in these conditions. Heading for Union Street, he remembered The Lemon Tree, where there was music in the bar on Friday nights—it might be worth looking in there, sometimes Em took her fiddle down to play with that crowd. She might only have mislaid her phone somewhere, everything might be all right.

He could hear the reel uncoiling from outside on the street; upstairs the place was full to bursting. Feeling conspicuous in his sombre coat with his laptop and briefcase, he pushed through to the inner bar, where it was the custom that the musicians simply sat around a table as part of the crowd. They didn't have any fixed programme for performing, either; someone started up and the others joined in when they were ready. Coming into the warmth from the frozen street, Alec was overwhelmed; he was no great enthusiast for traditional music, but tonight its intricate co-operations and skirl of desiring counteracted the nothingness of his lost days. Squeezing past the drinkers in the doorway, he saw Emmie at once, sawing away, bobbed hair flying against her hot cheeks, mouth settled in concentration, eyes on the others, following their lead. The reel was winding up, tighter and tighter.

What had he been afraid of? It was years since Em had done anything stupid. He had a moment's painterly vision of himself—more Caravaggio than Titian, picked out by yellow light in the crowded room, set apart as if he'd come back from the dead. Then the reel ended and Emmie lowered her bow; she saw him across the room and waved excitedly, smiling, beckoning him over.

In the Country

In a pile of other papers on the telephone table, there are two family photographs in an envelope: they are waiting for Julie to find frames for them. The Lavery family like to have photographs taken whenever they all get together. Both of these were posed in the same place in Stella's garden, in front of an old wall grown over with a rambler rose. In both, canvas chairs have been put out on the grass for the adults; the children are sitting on a rug. The photos were taken less than a year apart: the first one was Stella's sixtieth birthday and the roses are blooming, the second was Stella and Colin's thirty-fifth wedding anniversary, and the roses are only in bud. Someone looked it up and found that the thirty-fifth anniversary was jade, so they are all wearing something green; Stella begged to be excused horrible jade objects for presents (someone did buy them crème de menthe, for a joke). Stella and Colin are Ed's parents, Ed is Julie's husband. Mostly the same people are there in both photographs; the family composition has only crumbled slightly at the periphery. In the second picture Colin's elderly mother is missing, because she is in hospital with a broken ankle; also Ed's sister Cordelia has a different boyfriend. In the first picture Julie has two children, two boys. In the second picture she also has her new baby, another boy. He's too tiny to put on the rug, only a few weeks old. She is holding him almost ceremonially, upright against her chest. Her face is half hidden behind him, glancing away from the camera, as if she's dipping down to kiss his scented scalp, breathe into that mysterious black baby hair which will fall out after the first few weeks. Already, now that her baby is sitting up laughing fatly at his brothers, eating mashed banana, she's forgetting the secret of his first self: contained and pensive, with eyes as dark as blueberries, that seemed to know her.

*   *   *

When Ed and Julie drove into the yard on the morning of Stella's sixtieth, there seemed to be no one around, although the dog came strolling to greet them. They opened the car doors, the boys spilled out, Ed and Julie sat on in the car for a few more moments, subsiding after the stress of the journey from London. The peace of the place, at the end of a no-through-road, sifted on to them out of the air. Parts of the old farmhouse were fifteenth century or even earlier; in the stonework the whorls and arcs of lost doors and windows were preserved like fossils, and high in the walls of a ruined stone barn were the niches of a dovecot. Stella was an architect, she knew how to do nothing to spoil it all.

—Go and make sure the boys are safe, Julie said.

She got out and started unpacking the bags of presents and food, and their overnight things; they seemed to need such a huge quantity of stuff these days to go away anywhere. Ed in the passenger seat kept his eyes closed; because he was very long and thin and it was a small car he had to sit with his knees almost up to his chin. He wouldn't learn to drive. He groaned; he always managed to work himself up into a state of tension about these visits home. The dog, an intelligent old collie, pushed its

111

head sympathetically into his crotch. Julie walked around the barn and saw that the boys had found their cousins and that they were all with Colin, who was skimming weed off the pond with a net on a long handle; he waved at her. Beyond the garden Colin and Stella owned a couple of rough fields where she kept her horses and her goats, a copse of beeches, and a tiny two-roomed cottage at the bottom of the hill which she used as a studio and for overspill guests; the whole place was hidden away in the intricate folds of red sandstone Somerset hills, reached through lanes just wide enough for one car, between the high hedgerows that were ancient field boundaries. Julie had never stayed in the country in her childhood, but her imagination of it had been something like this.

The two double glass doors in the long room at the back of the house were flung wide open on to the paved terrace for the sunny day, but the curtains were pulled across inside, and Julie had to find a way through them; then her eyes took time adjusting to the thick, dim light. Stella was sitting on the sofa at one end of the room with her arms round her two daughters, Rose and Cordelia. They were watching television.

—Daytime television? Julie said. —Is this because now you're sixty you can let yourself go?

—Julie, darling, you've arrived! I didn't hear Tray barking. It's a DVD, Rose recorded it. Put it off, that's quite enough for now. It's rather hard to bear.

—No, let Julie see a bit of it.

—It's Mum, in her youth, said Rose. —She's about twenty, on some programme about what young people think. They were showing it as part of a 1960s season. She's on a panel. I just happened

112

to put it on and saw her on it: so we missed the beginning. It's amazing. She's so beautiful.

—I hardly remember doing the panel. I had no idea the footage still existed.

—It's when she was writing for *Spare Rib*.

—No, it's before *Spare Rib* existed.

—Look at her! Isn't she amazing?

Julie could never get used to how Stella's daughters were as intimate with their mother as puppies, always cuddling up and stroking and praising one another, confiding heated-up secrets or developing little tiffs. She had not known anything like this in her own family, although they didn't get on badly. In reaction she held herself back at a satirical cool distance, as if she and Stella were the grown-ups and Rose and Cordelia were lovable children.

They made room on the sofa for her to squeeze in. The film's washed-out colour made it look as if even the light and air were different in the past; Julie realised she was looking at a younger Stella. The girl on the television screen was wearing a paisley-patterned blouse and a fringed suede waistcoat. Her eyes were heavily made up and too dark for her pale perfect face, which was passionately in earnest; her long red-gold wavy hair seemed to crackle with static round her head. For the first moments it was shocking for Julie to connect that girl with the ageing woman beside her. 'I haven't actually taken LSD myself,' the girl said. 'But I can understand anyone dropping acid who isn't ready yet for an engagement with the system at the level of conflict.' Her voice was lighter and her accent seemed much more upper class than Stella's was now: she sounded like a well-brought-up schoolgirl on Speech Day. She wasn't

113

at all awkward with the cameras on her, although there was something polished and brittle about her defiance, as if it was the performance of a part.

—I was twenty-three, said Stella. —Is that any excuse? Did I really once sound that priggish? I refuse to believe it.

—It was you! Cordelia said. —You're just the same!

Stella turned the DVD player off although her daughters protested. —That's quite enough of that, she said. —Too lacerating. I want to play with my grandchildren. The day's too lovely. Where's Ed?

She stood up and began to haul back the heavy curtains from the windows. Stella at sixty was Julie's ideal of a certain kind of powerful older woman, tall and gaunt, with big bones; there was some pale peppery red colour left in the grey of the frizzy hair, which she still wore long, tied in a ponytail. As usual she was wearing baggy tracksuit bottoms with a man's shirt. Her pale freckled skin was beginning to be age-spotted and slackening on her bones; she was the type to be contemptuous of the idea of cosmetic surgery. Sometimes the nakedness of Stella's face dismayed Julie, sometimes she thought it was beautiful in its decay, like something she might have found in the woods round here, a piece of bark splotched over with lichen or a twiggy knot of witch's broom. She wondered if she would have the audacity, when the time came, to let herself go like that. She thought that you would have to think very well of yourself, to bear it.

Stella said something quickly and lightly while she and Julie were hitching up the curtains on the big brass hooks that caught them back: almost as if it was not for her daughters to hear. —How can it

114

be so long ago? It was only yesterday.

—It looked very interesting, Julie said carefully.

Ed came in, carrying bags. Whenever he first entered the family home he put on a face of nervous suffering which exasperated Julie, so that she kept her distance from him. —Happy birthday, Mother, he said, frowning and blinking: he called her Mother as if he was using the word ironically and it was too ordinary to be adequate to the history that lay between them. Ed was long and gangling like Stella, but he had Colin's eloquent brown eyes—dog eyes, Stella called them—and his expressive red full mouth, that seemed to twist up and down to express all varieties of distress and pleasure.

—My darling boy. Stella held her arms open for him; afterwards he submitted to his sisters' embraces.

—You and Julie are upstairs in the blue room, Stella said. —All the kids in the back attic. I've put Cordy and Seth down in the cottage. She thinks we'll be too much for him.

—Seth? Julie asked. —He's new. Is he nice?

—He's gorgeous, Stella said.

—No, he really is. I'm totally in love.

Cordelia had Colin's brown colouring too, and she was small and plump and soft-skinned like him.

—You'll recognise him when you see him, Rose said. —He's in a soap.

—Julie doesn't watch soaps, said Cordelia.

—Which one is he in? And where is he?

—*Emmerdale*. He's the doctor. And he's gone into Watchet for ciggies.

—Londoners can't seriously believe we don't have corner shops in the country.

—Really he's just trying to escape my clutches,

115

now I've dragged him down to meet my folks.

Julie walked down the garden to find out what the children were doing. Colin was organising all five of them—Rose had three, a boy and two girls—into a team at the pond, some skimming, some forking the weedy mess, Rose's smallest one importantly shooing the ducks, running at them waving little fat hands. When Julie saw they didn't need her she didn't approach any closer, she let herself drop down on to the rough grass. Unless for a moment she relaxed, she was never aware of being vigilantly on guard with Ed's family. Rolling over on to her face now, with her arms stretched out, she closed her eyes, and felt the hard shapes of the earth pressing up underneath her, unmoulded to her contours. She imagined being buried, having earth in her mouth and nose and ears, insects tickling over her, her flesh turning to a dry brown fertilising cake.

*   *   *

The men carried out the huge table that was cut from a single piece of oak, and put it on the grass under the apple trees: the double doors had deliberately been made wide enough for this. They brought out the most comfortable armchair, too, for Colin's mum, who was tiny, ancient, perplexed and deaf; everyone took turns to sit and chat with her. The dog lay under the table and the women spread out a cloth and put out dishes and flowers; Colin opened some white wine. He had found something special for the occasion because Stella didn't like champagne; Julie didn't know anything about wine, but she loved the zinging hit of the first mouthful out of the cold heavy glass. She put the glass down very carefully away from the edge of the table. All the ordinary things at Stella and Colin's—glasses, table napkins, carving knife, milk jug—were desirable in a way that Julie hadn't been aware of as a possibility for household items before she came to this house; although Stella handled them without any fuss, and never talked about shopping. If you asked, it would turn out that these things had been bought when they were first married and living in Iran, or that they had been made by some gifted silver designer who had died since, or were in some other way singular and interesting.

Stella changed out of her jogging bottoms into a green linen dress which she wore with bare legs and sandals and long ropes of pearls. Her daughters crowded her, exclaiming over the pearls. She made a debunking face to Julie across their bent heads. —Don't you think pearls are awfully county? These were my mother's, I've never really worn them.

—They're worth a fortune, Rose said.

—You're wondering which one will get them when I'm dead.

They protested in horror. —We don't want your wretched pearls. We want you.

—You're a wicked old woman to say such a thing.

—Haven't I always told you she was wicked? Colin joined in complacently.

—I'll leave the pearls to Julie then.

They made Julie try them on. She sat still where she was on one of the canvas chairs, with one leg crossed over the other, while Rose dropped them, doubled up, over her head, still warm from Stella's neck. They all looked smiling at her. Ed was cross-legged some way off under an apple tree, squinting at her over his cigarette. Stella had

117

forbidden him to smoke within twenty yards of the house and he had paced the distance out; Cordelia's new boyfriend, Seth, had insisted he was happy to not smoke at all, though it was he who had driven in the first place to buy the cigarettes. Julie felt herself swallowing against the weight of the pearls.

—Well? Am I very Sloane?

It might be the wrong joke: perhaps the pearls were too good for that. The family Stella came from weren't the Sloane kind of posh. However, they were all looking at her kindly, appraisingly. She had changed out of her jeans for the birthday lunch, and put on a bright red halterneck dress in a clinging stretch material that crossed over and tied in a bow at the small of her back; when she packed it she had wondered if it might be the wrong thing to wear for an outdoor summer meal, but looking round now she was sure that they approved. She could read their eyes and see herself, she didn't need a mirror, but Rose, kind Rose, insisted on dragging her inside. —You have to be shown how lovely you are, she said. It was nice anyway, to be out of the sunshine for those few minutes, in the empty house. In the dim stone-flagged entrance hall their reflections swam at them out of a tarnished gilt-framed mirror; both of them shuddered in the cool. Julie was always wary, forced to contemplate herself head-on. She hadn't been expected, when she was a child, to look like anything special.

—Aren't you just perfect? See?

Not perfect, ears too big, forehead so high: but something that still surprised her, and which she imagined as if it was to do with keeping a balance, holding those long level eyes and the swing of dark short hair and the bare straight shoulders still, like holding liquid steady in a glass: it might spill out if you looked too carefully.

—And I can't believe you've had two babies, Rose said wistfully, putting her hand on Julie's flat stomach.

—Those great boys. I sometimes wonder, where did they come from? Julie twisted Rose's rope of red hair in her hand. —I wish I had this.

—And the freckles that go with it?

—All the lot.

She wound the pearls in with Rose's hair and piled it on top of her head.

—That's very clever, said Rose. —Veronese. I look like a Venetian courtesan. He liked his women ample.

Julie didn't have to ask who Veronese was: Ed had taken her to Venice twice. They went outside with Julie holding up Rose's hair to show everyone. Then Cordelia wanted pearls in her hair too, and Stella had to find hairpins. Cordelia took her top off, to show them she also had Veronese breasts.

—Which really means, she said, —no kind of breasts at all, just little triangular white mounds. Like a boy's. Like custards.

And it was true, her breasts did make Julie remember the ones in some of those huge old paintings, pink-nippled little custards, disproportionate to the goddesses' huge thighs and bottoms; not that anything about Cordelia was huge, she was petite and pliant. Colin took a photograph of his daughter sitting at the table under the apple trees with pearls in her hair and her top off; all this was before they'd even started the food. Julie stole a quick glance at Cordelia's boyfriend and he seemed to be taking it all in his stride, laughing and talking

119

and looking at her breasts quite frankly. After all, he was an actor, he and Cordelia had met in a play, they would be used to this kind of thing. Only Vera, old Mrs Lavery, who wasn't supposed to understand, seemed embarrassed by Cordelia's nakedness. — Is Cordy all right? she asked no one in particular. Seth was good-looking, dark-skinned with shoulder-length black wiry curls and a strong, compact torso: at first Julie thought he must be Asian, until she worked out from his name and something he said that he was Jewish. If anything, he was trying a bit too hard to charm everyone. Ivan, Rose's violinist husband, was so shy that no charm reached him, he sat locked into the private world of his talent (not such a great talent, Ed thought).

Coming up to the table while she was helping get all the children into their places, Ed said something extra-ordinary to Julie. —Don't take *your* top off, he said in an undertone, quite seriously, like an instruction: as if he had really thought she might be tempted to. Luckily no one except Julie noticed it.

—Put them away now, Cordy, Stella said, bringing out the meat on a plate. —I'd hate them to get splashed with gravy.

Stella and Cordelia were vegetarians, but Stella always cooked meat for the others: this time a leg of Exmoor lamb with garlic and rosemary, the skin crisp and salty and blackened, the inside pink. Julie was concentrating on getting Frankie, her three-year-old, to sit still in his chair. He was over-excited after a game where all the children had hurled themselves at top speed down a grassy slope on to an old mattress they had dragged out from one of the barns. Frankie's face was red and wet with sweat, and he was bouncing crazily and arhythmically in his seat. His cousin Laurence, the gang leader, aged eight, encouraged him from across the table.

—Hey, Frankie!

—Hey, Laurie!

—Frankie, you're a pain, said Ed.

Roland, his older son, who was more obedient, watched Frankie reproachfully. Laurence bounced hard too, Frankie wriggled out of Julie's grip to bounce again, Ivan pleaded with Laurence in an undertone in French. Ivan's mother was French, he and Rose were bringing the children up to be bilingual.

—Hey, Laurence! Stella was a loved grandmother but also fearsome, so that the children watched her carefully. —Stop *now*, matey, or you'll be sent inside.

Rose and Ivan blushed and suffered at the threat of punishment.

Stella assessed anxiously what she put on to Ed's plate. —Is it cooked?

—It's good, said Ed, eating hungrily: he loved his mother's food. He was relaxing into the family as usual now, after his initial stand-off. He sat next to Stella; Colin sat at the other end of the table between his daughters and his old mother. Vera had a white linen napkin tucked in under her chin. Seth was telling them funny stories about working for a theatre director Colin knew.

—So what's this I hear about you being on the telly, Mother? Ed said.

He and his sisters could get away with calling the television the telly, and watching all the worst programmes.

—You mustn't see it, darling, Stella said. —It would be bad for your Oedipus complex. The girls

121

tell me I'm very gorgeous.

—I'm immune, said Ed. —You're not my type. What is it that you're saying, on this programme?

—That's the real mystery. Coming out of what certainly looks like my mouth used to look, are all these words that I'm sure I've never spoken.

—Such as?

Stella forked up a piece of Persian spinach pancake. —How about: 'It's important not to exaggerate the importance of libertarian elements in the processes of revolution.'

—You didn't really say that?

—She did! said Cordelia. —And 'The future is on the streets of Paris and Berlin.'

—That's the question. Was it me? It *looked* like me. But I have no memory of ever owning any such statements. Yet I sounded so certain.

Ed took more of the potatoes roasted in olive oil. —You old Maoist you.

—It's easy to make fun, Stella said. —I don't know which is more desolating: thinking how wrong I was then, or thinking that now I don't believe in anything with that certainty. Nothing political, anyway. Nobody does, do they?

—I don't know what I believe, said Julie, and then thought that she had drunk enough wine, she ought to stop.

—What I can actually remember about making that programme has nothing to do with ideas.

—I thought you couldn't remember it at all, Rose said.

—It's coming back to me. But only that I was meeting someone afterwards. All the time we were hanging about in the studio, having our make-up done, frightening the bourgeoisie, I was on fire with the boy I was going to meet. The man. I suppose they were men, by then.

—Oh, Mum! You *were* wicked.

—Why did that stuff get saved in my memory, and not what I believed in?

—What she remembers out of that welter of revolutionary fervour is me, Colin suggested, triumphant, from down the table.

Stella shook her head. —Not you. It wasn't you.

Julie looked to see if Colin minded it not having been him, but he didn't seem to, he was still beaming proudly at Stella.

*   *   *

Before Stella brought out the summer pudding, Colin banged his glass with his knife as if he wanted to make a speech.

—Oh, must you? Stella said.

Julie had known Colin from the radio and television, presenting various arts programmes, years before she went out with Ed. His screen persona was hard and rigorous and exact; she was surprised when she met him by how soft and pleased with himself he seemed, as if he only taxed himself when he was performing. Contracted to fit the television, his handsome plump brown face and thick white hair intensified and deepened; in real life she found him inaccessible behind a vague easy friendliness, although he knew lots of interesting things.

—I'm going to sing, he announced, enjoying the chorus of groans. —For Stella's birthday.

—Oh God, said Ed to Stella. —Not his Geordie childhood, please.

123

—But I love the songs, Stella said.

When she and Colin were first married he was still a singer on the folk circuit.

—Sair fyeld hinny. That translates for you southerners as 'sore failed hinny'. Sair fyeld noo. 'Sore failed now, sore failed hinny, since I knew you.'

—Cheerful, said Cordelia.

—It's a poignant lament for lost youth. An old man sings it to an oak tree.

—Oh dear. Vera smiled round the table in wonder at her clever son.

—To an oak tree? I thought hinny was a girl. His girlfriend.

—Well, that's what he calls the old oak tree. It's an endearment.

Colin's voice was still good, strong and velvety, and he sang without any affectation, not putting on the folk style that he had learned in his youth. It made a good moment, the family assembled in the long grass of the orchard under the apple trees, all lightly drunk on the white wine, the children drunk from their play, the song in its power drawing the meaning of the day together, looping them all into one true feeling that cleared their heads for more spacious and open thoughts.

Aa was young and lusty aa was fair and clear
Aa was young and lusty many's a long year
When I was five and twenty a could loup a dyke
Noo a'm five and sixty aa can barely step a syke.

Thus spoke the ould man to the oak tree
Sair fyeld is aa sin a kenned thee!

Julie caught the eye of Cordelia's boyfriend and knew that he was watching them all, uncertain how to fit in with this family and their unashamed grand gestures.

—Do you remember that one, Nana? Ed called to Vera down the table. —Did you use to sing that up in Newcastle when Dad was a kid?

—I don't think so, pet, said Vera vaguely.

Later, when the children had gone off with Stella to feed the horses, and Julie and Ed were stacking the dishes from the table in a big basket to carry into the kitchen, Ed put his arms around her from behind, and kissed her on her back, naked where her dress plunged down. 'Aa was young and lusty many's a long year,' he imitated, muffled against her skin, so that she knew he had been listening to his father even though he had pretended only to be weary at his showing off. She also knew that he was apologising for his moodiness earlier, and perhaps for the remark about taking her top off, although he might have just thought that was sensible advice. She wasn't really angry with him; she had talked with Stella about how it was difficult for Ed, trying to make a career as a critic and writer and trying to do it differently to Colin—Ed wanted to be more subtle, more sceptical, less ripe—but always having to operate in the blurring broad shadow of his father. It was no wonder he behaved badly sometimes, returned into his parents' orbit.

* * *

At the end of the afternoon Julie went for a walk by herself. The curtains were pulled shut across the windows in the living room again, and the children

125

were watching a film, something Colin had been sent that was only just out in the cinemas. Stella and Cordelia had taken the horses out, Rose was with the children, Ivan was practising, Ed and Colin both had articles to finish. Julie had only meant to step outside for a few minutes, but once she began to walk down the path that led along the fields and through the copse of beech trees, there seemed no reason to turn back; they could all manage without her for half an hour. Alone, she felt returned with intensity inside herself, aware of the breathing lifting her chest and the suddenly awakened noise of her thoughts rushing in the hollow of her skull. Yellow light slanted low across the path from between the trees; little birds scuffled in the undergrowth or flitted among the leaves like tricks of sight. A wood pigeon took off from a branch with a startling racket, its wingbeats like shots. It was a lovely English summer's afternoon: she had longed to escape into it, but as she walked it remained outside of her, as if she was walking through a commercial, or an estate agent's brochure.

Stella and Colin weren't really country people. Ten years ago, not long before Julie first met them, they had given up their London life. Julie and Ed lived now in the converted bottom half of the tall Georgian terraced house in Highbury that had been Ed's childhood home; the top half was let out and the rents went to Rose and Cordelia. As she walked Julie was thinking about the way the young Stella on the television programme had talked about revolution, speaking the word as if it was a knife kept hidden under her clothes, gleaming and glamorous; she could imagine nursing that hope of some violent adjustment, recharging life with its truth. Sometimes Julie was afraid of how experience

126

now seemed thin and used up, as if her children were the only real thing. Because terrible things happening in other places were so close, on the television and the Internet and in the newspapers, even the solidity of these old hills and woods could seem worn paper-thin. Outwardly the countryside looked the same as it did a hundred years ago, as if there was a wholesome continuity preserved here, safe against change; but that was a delusion. For a start, all the cottages that must have once belonged to poor people were done up now and sold for a fortune to people from the cities.

She was nervous when she heard the noise of someone else moving in the woods behind her, twigs cracking underfoot; probably it was someone from the village walking their dog. She should have brought Tray, too, as a pretext for being here: only she'd slipped away without meaning to come more than a few yards. Looking back she saw Seth, the actor, approaching along the path, his white T-shirt flickering in the shade; he called out and waved to her, and she waited, feeling the sun hot on her in a patch of light where trees had been cut down. After lunch she had put on one of Ed's shirts over her dress and she had been glad of it in the cool of the copse. She was pleased to have Seth's company; as he came close her sour thoughts drew off some little distance, as if he was surrounded with a stronger force of pleasurable energy; when he asked if he could get through to the cottage this way, she said she would show him. Because he wore his black hair in a glossy mass to his shoulders, his looks reminded her of the Assyrian kings in the lion hunts she'd taken the boys to see in the British Museum; he had the same slanting cheekbones, although instead of warrior-like he was funny and friendly. He wasn't much taller than she was, not six foot; around one wrist, she noticed, he wore a gold chain, and the brown skin of his arms was speckled with dark pores; he had a warm male smell she enjoyed, like hazelnut oil. He explained that he'd thought he ought to take a couple of hours out, he had some lines to learn. They walked on together through the trees, and then along the side of a field planted with tall elephant grass for biofuel. Seth said he'd thought it was wheat. —Shit, I've hardly ever been in the country before. What are those? He pointed to some sheep in the next field. —Cows? Rabbits?

—Come on, you must have been to the country. At least as a kid, on a trip or something.

—I've always been meaning to get round to it.

—It's lovely here, she said. —Look at the view.

The view from the top of the field really was good, they could see all round them: the sea behind, Exmoor to the south, and close at hand the patched cloth of little ancient fields, some worn into a corduroy of ridged sheep runs, draped across a relief of steep hills and valleys so convoluted that Julie was never sure which hamlet or which woods she was looking at, although she came here often. They dropped to sit beside the Dutch barn, with a few bleached hay bales left over in it from last year. Julie knew that an unspoken alliance between them had begun at lunch, when their eyes met over Colin's song, the outsiders in the family. Seth smoked a cigarette. —I was too frightened to smoke at the house, he said. —Cordy's old lady's fairly intimidating.

—Do you see the cottage from here? Julie said. —But I'll come down with you, it's on my way back.

—I really just wanted to clear my head, he said. —I'll probably just fall asleep over my script anyway.

—Is this *Emmerdale*? she said. —Are you really the doctor?

—There I was thinking you might be a fan.

—Perhaps I'll watch it now, just to see you.

—Do me a favour. I'd rather you didn't. It's so funny. I've just broken up with my girlfriend.

—You don't mean Cordelia?

—On *Emmerdale*. The actress was already in Australia when they decided to write her out, so we couldn't actually have the break-up, I had to do it on the phone, only of course there wasn't anyone on the other end, it was only me all by myself, ranting into nothingness. 'What do you mean, you think I haven't made enough commitment to this relationship?' 'How can you say that I'm a selfish bastard who only cares about his work?'

Lying on his back on the stony margin of the field he laughed delightedly, and she laughed too.

—What do you do, Julie? When you're not at home with the kids?

—At the moment mostly I'm at home with them.

—They're nice—pretty girls.

—Boys. Mine are the boys. The girls are Rose's.

—Shit. I'm hopeless with kids.

—Why shouldn't you be? she said tolerantly. —I do a bit of freelance accountancy work for small charities, because Ed isn't earning much from his writing at the moment. When Ed and I were first together I was working as a PA for a Japanese importer. I don't think he'd ever met anyone before who hadn't been to university.

—They are a bit overwhelming: the family.

—I love them, Julie said. —I really do love them.

129

—God, I said some idiotic things to Cordy's father over that lunch.

—It won't matter. But you should always keep something of yourself back from them. Keep a few secrets.

Seth propped himself up on his elbows to look at her.

—Is that what you do?

—Just in case they accept everything about you.

—That would be bad?

—I'm just superstitious.

—What sort of secrets? he asked, and she laughed at him.

—Now, why would I tell you?

She stood up, brushing bits of straw off her dress, and they made their way down the side of a stubble field, treading sweetness from the camomile plants that crept underfoot; below them the slate roof of the cottage glinted through a sliver of woodland, where the last of the slanting sun touched the valley bottom. When they stepped in under the trees the light was thick and green; the path followed beside a stream sunk to a summer trickle among mossy stones. The different acoustic in the wood made Julie shiver, as if she could feel the noise of their steps and their breathing, on her skin stretched taut.

—Ed knows, for instance, Julie said, —that before I knew him I used to be a Christian. But he doesn't know quite how much of one.

—That's all?

—Really an extreme kind of a Christian. I ran away from home and lived with an evangelical group for about a year. I was engaged to one of them. Quite a crazy kind of group. The women all had to cover their heads with scarves, and only the men were allowed to take prayer at the meetings. The women had to obey the men, and the men had to obey the leaders of the group. The elders, we called them. All the money we earned was collected centrally, we were given allowances.

—You're joking. This was you?

—Amazing, isn't it? Where did that money go? When I think about it now. I was temping in an insurance office: I put in all my wages. Those men who ran the group and the whole hierarchy were completely unelected, there were no checks on them, we never knew how they were chosen, it was a process hidden from us, we didn't question it. We went to lectures proving that evolution didn't happen, that God created the world in seven days.

—Surely Ed's heard about all this stuff when he's talked to your parents?

—My parents don't know the half of what went on. Also, they don't get together with Ed's family very often. They're shy people. They don't talk about very much.

—And what happened? How did you get out?

—It wasn't a prison, we were there of our free choice. I just walked away. Well, actually I caught a train.

The last few yards were a rocky scramble; their feet skidded, sending stones rattling; there was still thick sunlight on the track when they came out beside the white-painted cottage wall.

—I haven't talked to anybody about all that for years, said Julie.

—Do you fancy a beer? he said. —There are some in the fridge. The key's under a brick. Cordy says there is no crime round here. Or perhaps just

131

very thick burglars. Otherwise why hide the key at all?

* * *

On the ground floor of the cottage there was just one room, with a fridge and sink and cooker and a bed; upstairs was Stella's studio. Seth took the top off a bottle of cold beer for Julie then excused himself and went into the tiny bathroom. She sat down on the bed and took in Cordelia's occupation of the space: her holdall on the bed with clothes half pulled out of it, a couple of paperbacks with their spines broken and pages furred, her iPod charging, a grubby make-up bag beside the sink spilling over with lipsticks, medicines, contraceptive pills, perfume. The way Cordelia allowed her intimate life to flow over and fill any given space struck Julie as unprotected, childlike, dangerous. The only signs of Seth were a masculine heap of keys and wallet and change emptied from his pocket, and a white jacket on a hanger on a cupboard door. The duvet on the bed was still pulled up over the pillows; they had only arrived this morning. The cottage was all in shadow; its perfunctory furnishings seemed a flimsy shell against the light outside the windows.

When Seth came out of the bathroom he showed Julie a little polythene packet.

—Do you fancy a little bit of charlie?

She hadn't touched any drugs since she was pregnant with Roland, and she'd only ever done coke a few times at parties. —I don't think so.

—We bought it specially for the weekend. I thought this might be a good moment.

—Or maybe, Julie said. —Just a little bit. You

132

go first.

He sat on a rickety cane chair opposite her and put out the lines with a credit card from his wallet, on the cover of a book of British birds; she worried shyly that she might make a mess of doing it after all this time, but copied him exactly and remembered how.

—Nice, he said, sitting back with his eyes gleaming at her, pressing the back of his brown wrist against his nostril. —It's decent stuff.

Julie felt the blooming of intoxication at the front of her mind like a flare, and breathed cold air in sharply. —I'd forgotten what it was like.

—About that sect, he said. —That's fantastic. You weren't making all that up?

—No: why would I?

—It's just very hard to imagine you. You don't look the type.

Julie was inspired to show him: she buttoned Ed's shirt up to the neck. She wasn't sure how affected she was by the coke—she'd only had a small amount, but she wasn't used to it, so she stood up cautiously, conscious of herself swaying, not unsteadily but heavily and flexibly, like a tree. All the emptiness she had felt when she was walking alone had vanished; she was densely concentrated in the present. The understanding came to her that these alternating moods were two pulses in life, opposite and yet related, like the expansion and contraction of a heartbeat: one diffusing sensation and sending it flying apart, this one gathering it in to the living centre. She had noticed a blue tea towel folded by the sink; shaking it out she arranged it neatly over her hair, folding it across her forehead and tucking it behind her ears

133

with accustomed fingers. It wasn't quite big enough to make a proper headscarf but it wasn't bad.

Seth appraised her, sprawling and tipping on the little chair, one arm across its back. —I like it.

She sat down opposite him again, on the side of the bed. Their knees touched.

—You have to imagine the kind of sex life I was having with this man: 'my betrothed'. They used all this phoney biblical language. He was thirty, I was seventeen. Of course sexual intercourse before marriage was forbidden. The way he interpreted that was that we could do everything else except for actually fucking. And then afterwards, when we'd worked ourselves up into a fine state, we had to pray together.

—You're kidding.

—Like this. She put her hands together on her lap, bent her covered head, and dropped her eyes; for a few moments she focused deeply, making herself sorrowful and troubled. She was conscious through her knees of Seth's holding himself intently still, she thought she could feel the thudding in his chest.

—Lord, look into my heart, she said in a low voice, urgently. —You know what I am, you know how much sin there is in me.

*   *   *

Once, afterwards, when the boys were at school and nursery and Ed was out, Julie watched Seth on television, in his soap. She couldn't actually sit and watch it concentratedly, she had to be doing something else; she set up the ironing board in front of the television and brought in a pile of Ed's

134

shirts and the boys' clothes to get on with. Seth only appeared briefly in a storyline in the first part of that episode, so she spent most of it keyed up in an anticipation that came to nothing. When the credits rolled and she saw his name she doubled up with a peculiar hollow pain in her abdomen, and then she made herself hold the hot tip of the iron just for a long moment against the skin on the back of her wrist; it raised an ugly blister which didn't heal for weeks, and left a little V-shaped scar. She was feeling all sorts of odd things around that time anyway, early in her pregnancy. After that she didn't ever watch it again, and then later she heard that he'd left *Emmerdale*, and was getting decent parts in the theatre instead.

He and Cordelia split up, fairly amicably. Julie had known that was going to happen, partly from things he said, and partly from the sight of that heap of his keys and money left like a provisional small island in the sea of Cordelia's things. Nothing changed in Cordelia's attitude to Julie, so presumably Seth hadn't told her anything. He telephoned Julie once, after he'd finished with Cordelia, but she said she didn't want to see him. She told Ed that Seth had phoned, because she wanted to mention him aloud; she pretended that he'd wanted a number for a contact they'd mentioned to him over that weekend in Somerset. Ed said he thought it was a bit much.

When Julie had got back to the farmhouse on that evening of Stella's birthday, Stella and Cordelia were just riding into the yard: she stood for a while in the dusk while they dismounted, exultant from their exercise, in the romance of the hot smell of the horses and their stiff-legged sideways dancing, hooves clattering and striking

135

sparks from the cobbles. Rose was dozing inside on the sofa, the film had finished, the children were squabbling and watching cartoons; it was long past Frankie's bedtime, but Rose's children were never put to bed anyway until they fell asleep where they were. No one had even noticed that Julie had gone out. Stella put soup and bread and cheese and home-made chutney on to the oak table; while they were eating Seth came in from learning his lines at the cottage. He and Julie had carried the evening off with perfect calm.

Cordelia said she couldn't keep awake after her ride; she yawned and huddled into an old dressing-gown of Colin's. She put her feet on to Seth's lap and asked him to rub them. The Laverys liked playing games on family occasions: when the younger children were finally asleep the grown-ups first played *Ex Libris,* which was about guessing the first or last sentences of novels, and then the game where everyone writes the names of ten famous people, real or invented, and mixes them up in a saucepan. Cordelia wouldn't play. Julie felt joyous all evening, although she didn't usually like games. She and Seth were on the same team; whatever clues he gave about the names he got, she seemed to be able to guess them straight away. She took Roland outside to show him the moon while Seth and Ed were rolling up and smoking in the dark garden. Roland was in his pyjamas, he complained that the grass was making his feet wet; she lifted him up on to her hip, although he was seven years old and getting too heavy for her to carry. She could smell rank marijuana; in the dark the child's body hot and heavy against hers seemed to be part of the unfolding sensation of the man's weight against her earlier. That evening all the ordinary things that she and Seth said to one another, all the times they brushed past each other or sat down together, were a code for something else enormously important that had happened, but did not appear.

The Godchildren

The three heirs, in three separate taxis, converged on 33 Everdene Walk on a fine afternoon in late May. They were in their early fifties and had not met since they were sixteen or seventeen. Amanda, who had been officious even as a teenager, had organised the meeting by email, via the solicitors: —If we're all going to the house, why don't we go at the same time? Wouldn't it be fun to meet up?

Now each was regretting having agreed to this.

Chris, who was a lecturer at a new university, was certain he had spotted Amanda at the station, ahead of him in the queue for taxis; he had been too embarrassed to make himself known to her, even though they could have shared the fare. She surely hadn't had all that red hair thirty-five years ago, and she hadn't seemed so tall then, or so loosely put together: the woman in the queue wasn't large exactly, but physically complicated, with a bright-coloured striped wrap tossed over one shoulder which made him think of beachwear. Perhaps she lived in a hot country. He'd only recognised her when she threw her unguarded, emphatic glance at everyone behind her in the queue—boldly but blindly. Quailing, Chris was suddenly his anguished seventeen-year-old self again, stripped of his disguise as someone experienced and distinguished. His memories of Mandy, young, were dim but had an ominous intensity. He wished he hadn't come. He knew already that he wouldn't want anything, anyway, from the horrible old house. At least he wouldn't be alone with Amanda; although when he tried to recover his memories of Susan, the other godchild, he couldn't find anything at all, only a neatly labelled vacancy.

The three taxis bore them, just a few minutes apart, out of the city centre, then, swooping decorously downhill between traffic lights, through a species of suburb that seemed more remote from their present lives than anywhere they ever went on holiday. The sleepy wide road was lined with limes, then flowering cherries; they passed a little brick-built library, a church, discreetly evangelical. Infantile knee-high white-painted gates opened on to bungalow gardens smothering under the pink and white foam of weigela and flowering currant, waterfalls of clematis; the semi-detached house fronts were festooned with nostalgic wisteria. Four-by-fours were drawn up off the road, on asphalted drives. The sun shone unfalteringly, embalming everything; seeds and pollen drifted sidelong in the motionless air. What it brought back was not so much their past as a past beyond their past. By the time these three had come as children to visit their godmother here, their more fashionable parents had already decided that the suburbs were dreary: places to joke about, not to aspire to. Their parents were doing up, in those days, spindly dilapidated eighteenth-century houses, bought cheap, in the city centre. Susan's mother still lived in one of these, now worth a great deal, and Susan had spent the previous night in her childhood bed. In her taxi, she was hardly thinking of the meeting ahead—except to wish that she weren't going to it. She was obsessing over jagged old irritations, roused by a conversation with her mother that morning.

139

Chris's and Susan's taxis pulled up outside 33 Everdene Walk at the same moment; Amanda had got there before them, and the front door stood open upon what seemed to their foreboding a seething blackness, in contrast to the glare outside. Who knew what state the house would be in? Susan was quicker, paying her taxi off; Chris was always afraid that he would tip too little or too much. She looked away while he probed in his change purse, then they politely pretended to recognise each other. He tried to dig back in his mind to their old acquaintance: how hadn't he seen that the invisible unremembered Susan might grow into this slim, long-faced, long-legged dark woman, somewhat ravaged but contained and elegant?

Meanwhile, Amanda, watching from a window she had just opened upstairs, saw thirty-five years of change heaped in one awful moment on both their heads. They looked broken-down to her, appalling. On her way to the house, she had bullied her resisting taxi driver into two consecutive U-turns between the lime trees: visited by a premonition of just this disappointment, and then recovering, repressing her dread, willing herself to hope. Amanda remembered the old days more vividly than either of the others, cherished the idea of their shared past—strangely, because at the time she had seemed the one most ready to trample it underfoot, on her way to better things. Now she revolted at Chris's untidy grey-white locks, windswept without wind, around his bald patch: why did men yield so readily to their disintegration? At least Susan had the decency to keep her hair brown and well cut. Chris was stooping and bobbing at Susan, smiling lopsidedly, self-deprecatory. He wound one foot behind the other calf, rubbing his shoe on his trouser leg; when he'd done that at seventeen, it had seemed to Amanda a sign of a tormented sensibility, which she had ached to explore and conquer.

She whistled from the window, piercing the Walk's tranquillity.

—Come on up! she shouted. —Prepare for the Chamber of Horrors!

*   *   *

Not only the air inside the house but the light, from forty-watt bulbs, seemed ancient and rotten. The curtains were drawn across the windows in all the rooms. Odds and ends of furniture—a folding card table, a standard lamp, a barometer, picture frames showing peeling strips of passepartout— were piled in the hall, half sorted, inventoried, forlorn and sour with damp. The house had been empty for a year, from the time of their godmother Vivien's death. But none of the three had visited it since long before that, when they were teenagers and came together. Chris had fallen out of touch with Vivien completely, decades earlier, on political grounds, and because it had never occurred to him that he owed her any duty; Amanda and Susan had seen her occasionally in London over the years—separately, and not recently.

Susan stopped abruptly in the hall.

—But it's so tiny! she said. —Was it always this size? How come I remember it as spacious?

—I don't remember anything, Chris said, alarmed. —Is it some form of dementia? I thought

I remembered the house, but I'd swear I've never set foot in here before.

—I've got rid of the solicitor, Amanda called from somewhere over their heads. —We've got it all to ourselves. I said we'd return the key to him when we finished. He was glad to get out—who can blame him? Isn't it horrid? They'll never sell it, will they?

A squat staircase crawled up one wall from the varnished parquet in the hall; at the top, three bedrooms opened off a landing, along with a toilet and a bathroom whose stains they shuddered at. Amanda loomed in a doorway: years ago, the striped thing draped across her shoulder would have been called a poncho. Her voice was more familiar to Chris and Susan than her person: caramel, hectoring, running on and on. What they both remembered most clearly—though differently—about the young Mandy was her physical perfection, as simple as a drawing done in a single curving line. Whatever she had worn in those days—a dress, or jeans and a T-shirt—had suggested her stepping out of it in one smooth movement. Her ease in her own body had been morally terrifying to the others. Her face was still bright—she had good skin and a thick mane of hair—but the rest of her had grown overbearing, to match her voice. Now she wore flat shoes and harem pants and a lot of jewellery.

Amanda had brought a packet of coloured stickers. The plan for today, devised by her, was that they should each choose a colour and put stickers on any items they wanted, then go shares on a man with a van to collect it all and deliver it to their respective homes. They had been invited to take whatever they liked from the house. They had also been left quite a few thousand pounds each, from a trust fund. This had come as a pleasant surprise to Chris, who was genuinely not worldly enough to have thought of the possibility, and had pretty much forgotten that he had a godmother. None of them were heir to the property itself, which had gone to a niece and a nephew, deserving because they had been kind to Vivien in her old age.

—Oh, is this her? Chris picked up a photograph from the top of a chest of drawers, where it was arranged on a lace doily along with a tin alarm clock and a cut-glass dish full of buttons and paper clips, everything soft with dust. —The face does ring a bell. He was reassured. —She's starting to come back to me.

In the photograph, Vivien wore a checked dress with a Peter Pan collar. Her small laughing eyes, horsy long jaw, and exuberant big-toothed smile were sandwiched between two circles of glass, held in a base of faded art deco plastic.

—Somehow she persuaded us she was good-looking, Amanda said. —She used to seem so glamorous.

Susan crossed to the open window, as if to breathe. —This place is giving me the creeps. I don't want anything.

—Don't be silly, Amanda said. —Take it and sell it on eBay.

—It's all old junk. Nothing's even antique.

—You'll be surprised what you can get for it.

Susan was fishing in her handbag. —I'm going to call the cab back. This was a mistake. Sorry, Mandy. I've had a dreadful morning with my mother.

143

Amanda, focusing, took in properly for the first time that Susan's understated bag was made of leather as soft as cloth, and that her clothes were sumptuous: simple cream linen dress, cranberry-red cashmere cardigan over her shoulders.

—Actually, it's giving me the creeps, too, Chris said, looking nervously from one woman to the other. —I could use a cab—if you don't mind sharing, Susan?

—Oh, no! Amanda wailed. —You pigs! You can't leave me here on my own. It's not fair!

Chris and Susan stared at this overflowing stranger, claiming them. Both felt an inappropriate anxiety that she might howl with tears, and they might be held unjustly to blame for it.

—Please, she said, softening. —We can do the stickers later. We could go out in the garden; we could find a local pub. But we can't just let one another go as easily as that, as if none of it meant anything. Can we?

Chris was bewildered. —None of what?

*   *   *

It wasn't anything sinister or criminal. Every few months, year after year, Vivien's daddy, who was tiny, bulky-shouldered, ill-tempered, with a burnished, age-spotted bald pate, had picked them up in his car from their respective houses and driven them to Everdene Walk in a grim silence that was almost hieratic, as if they were sacrifices heaped up for his daughter visiting from London, where she worked as a PA to a succession of managers at ITN and Granada. From his driver's seat, Daddy had emanated the distaste of a serious man for the frivolity of children,

144

and an alarm that they might somehow damage his beige leather upholstery. But Vivien had been lovely to them, in her way. She had no children of her own: this was what their parents had always said when handing them over, as though they were being sent to soak up some surplus of mothering that childless women couldn't help secreting. But Vivien wasn't mother-like at all. She had not married, and Amanda and Susan learned only later—Chris never knew about it, because he wasn't interested—of her lifelong love affair with a married man in London. By the time of the children's visits, whatever friendship had originally made each set of parents choose Vivien as a godmother had melted away: Vivien was too bossy, she was a snob, she belonged to a world of musty charm and optimism that their parents were leaving behind in the 1960s. The parents had been apologetic, actually, when Daddy's car came, for sending their children as their proxies, when they were too bored to go themselves. But the children hadn't minded, and not only because of the treats.

—None of what? Chris asked, afraid that he'd missed something.

—Us! Amanda swept her arm to indicate the three of them, the sleeve of her poncho catching in a wickerwork pagoda on a side table. —We were really close, weren't we? We were three odd solitary kids and we didn't make friends easily, but here we met without any baggage, and we got on. It meant a lot to me.

Sometimes Amanda reread old volumes of her diary; she still wrote in it too, filling pages copiously when things weren't going well.

The others were accusing. —You weren't solitary.

—I was the most solitary of all: at least you both had brothers and sisters.

—You were awfully spoiled, Susan said, —with your ballet lessons and your deportment lessons and your tennis.

—I didn't ever have deportment lessons. Look, are you two going to stay? Don't let me down!

Susan stood hesitating. It depended on her: the others saw her power, which they hadn't noticed in the old days. Her face was haggard, cheekbones jutting above hollows: if it was beautiful, there was also something naked in it, shocking. The unblemished skin was textured like soft parchment. What Amanda remembered was glasses, a flat chest, hand-me-down bobbled jumpers (Amanda had refused to wear hers, once the wool went like that), a reputation for good marks at the school where she had a scholarship (not the school that Amanda's parents paid for), and a stubborn, sulking resistance to Amanda, who—used to capitulation—had been intrigued.

—There's a lot of Chinese stuff here, Chris said, disentangling the pagoda from the poncho.

—They lived in Singapore when she was little, and then Paris. That's where they got their international flavour. You'd have thought they were jet-setters, from the way they talked. But Daddy was only in insurance.

Warily Susan dropped her mobile back in her bag, yielding as if she didn't do it often.

—All right then, she said. —I'll stay for a bit. For old times' sake.

In the decaying room, the three of them were linked in heady intimacy for a moment, though they were also strangers.

146

—I'll stay as well, Chris said.
But the women had taken this for granted.

*   *   *

They found their old den. The others had forgotten
it, but Amanda remembered and led them to it—
bearing bottles raided from the kitchen—though
the way through the garden was unrecognisable.
This garden had once been Daddy's pride:
amoeba-shaped flower beds mounded with colour,
crazy-paving paths set in close-clipped lawns. There
had been a swinging lounge seat with a striped
awning, and every summer's day had revolved
around the necessity of taking this awning in if rain
threatened. Now the neighbours in the Walk must
have been despairing at the incursion of wilderness
into their sanctuary: rusty dock and nettle stood
waist high, bramble was advancing in the tall grass.
Rubbish had been thrown in here, split bags bulging
with rot, a spillage of broken things from the house,
a plastic clotheshorse, a smashed china bread crock.
In the heat, it all smelled potently of rank growth,
baked earth, dog shit. The den was lifted up above
the chaos, a raised space of hard mud on a bank
among trees at the far end of the garden, opposite
Vivien's bedroom window, backing on to a little
copse where the locals walked their dogs.
Susan had brought a blanket from the house for
them to sit on, and Amanda had chocolate in her
handbag. They examined more closely the bottles
they'd liberated: Johnnie Walker, Tia Maria,
Cinzano, amontillado sherry. The bottles were
filthy, sticky, greasy, but Amanda was adamant that
the alcohol was safe. She wiped around the tops

with tissues soaked in whisky, and was the first to swig, choosing the sherry. —My favourite, she said. —Goes straight to your head. Wow!

—Out here I feel more relaxed, said Susan. Lying back on the blanket, she looked up at the blue sky through the spreading fans of leaves in a silver birch, wafting in the merest movement of air. The urgent onward flow of her days ceased abruptly; the sensation was as if something—her soul—had floated to the front of her forehead, while she sank down, breathing differently, vastly. —That's what used to happen, in the old days. We used to get away from the house, out here.

—But not at first. At first we loved it all.

Vivien used to have tea ready for them when they came: Twiglets, sandwiches with the crusts cut off, cream cakes, ice cream, jelly. If they visited her in London, she took them to the opera at Covent Garden, the Natural History Museum, the Mermaid Theatre, Chez Solange—where a waiter picked extra strawberries off a gateau for Amanda.

Chris played it safe with the Johnnie Walker. Susan tried Cinzano, in memory of Vivien. She reported that it was hideous.

—I danced for you all in this garden, Amanda said.

Chris seemed to see her, in a leotard and some sort of scanty, fancy-painted yellow nylon thing, fastened to elastic on her wrists, which she waved about like wings. He remembered registering both her absurd self-importance and self-exposure (the dancing wasn't very good) and the breath-stopping effect of her bare creamy legs and bouncing pyramids of breast.

They had all shown off. Vivien had encouraged

them to do it. Mandy had been a beauty, Chris a genius—he had held forth on existentialism, on the problem with Communism, which was human nature. They tried to think what Susan had been: Susan had had personality and depth, they remembered. She had read Dickens when she was eleven. Licensed, leaving shame behind them in the real world, they had expanded into the place Vivien made for them, reinventing themselves, becoming in the free space of the Walk exceptional. They had talked together, even in front of Vivien, as they talked to none of their friends, confessing their aspirations and their real thoughts.

Invited into Vivien's bedroom, the girls had watched her change with skilful minimal movements into something pretty, tipping a bottle, dabbing perfume on pressure points, fixing earrings, skewering her feet into high heels. She had had a neat, miniature figure, had been quick and lithe and always on the move, talking and organising. She had lent them novels—Nancy Mitford and Dodie Smith—and showed them photographs of Paris. Sweet as cake with them, she'd shown herself flinty towards anything she didn't approve of. She couldn't bear the hordes of tourists overtaking her old favourite places in France; she couldn't bear the greed of the trade unions, or sloppy language— split infinitives or Bristol accents. The children hardly spoke to their parents about what went on at Vivien's, fearing the chill of a different judgement than hers, a condemnation of her fakery.

—I didn't need deportment classes, Amanda said. —I had natural deportment—don't you remember Vivien saying that? Natural deportment. And look what's become of me!

149

—What has become of you?

—Two shops selling ethnic jewellery: Weymouth and Bridport. What about you?

—I'm in family law. I work on contract to social services.

Vivien had been right about Chris, though, Amanda said. She'd looked him up on his university website: he was a professor of Early Modern Studies, whatever those were; he'd written books. With ready irony (this was a sensitive subject), he explained that at his university 'professor' was only an honorary title; it didn't mean what it did at the old universities—no promotion, no extra salary. Not even much honour, really. Also, nobody read his books.

—Did she ever mention God? Susan said lazily, not sitting up. —After all, we were her godchildren.

—She gave me a little white Testament when I was confirmed, Amanda said. —I still have it, but I've never read it.

*   *   *

When they were drunk enough, they returned to the house. It seemed even chillier and dirtier inside, after their soak in the afternoon light. The kitchen hadn't been altered in decades: there was an old gas stove, an enamel sink, little gingham curtains in place of cupboard doors. Bone-china tea sets had been pulled out of the cupboards and piled on the table with colander, grater, mincer, wooden spoons anciently dark, Breton bowls painted with names, not theirs. They felt as if they'd come upon the scene of a desecrating burglary.

—We might as well take this stuff, Amanda said,

pressing her stickers defiantly on to a few items— jugs and serving dishes—and piling them apart from the rest. —You know they'll only get the clearance people in.

—I liked this house so much, Susan said. —I liked it better than my own house, though I knew I shouldn't. I didn't like modern things. I liked the thick pink carpet and the embroidered tablecloths—they were like something out of books. I imagined having flowers on the breakfast table and a maid to turn back your bed. Not that Vivien had maids. But in those days I thought I'd want to live like that. In my head, I lived like that.

—Have a tablecloth. Here's a whole pile of them.

—Now it all looks dismal.

—Did you go and see her, when she was ill?

None of them had. To be fair, they had not known how ill she was. Amanda and Susan had spoken to her on the phone, in the last year; Vivien, who had never allowed herself to be ill for a day— as if it were a lapse in taste—had complained in angry spurts, between deploring her weakness for doing so, about her legs and her eyes. They had never been in touch with the niece or the nephew, so had not known that anything was serious, or terminal. They had known from Vivien's voice, however, that she was changed, desperate, and they had not done anything about it. The married man— news trickled through to their parents, always months late—had also been very ill, then died. — It's our punishment, Susan said. —To be here.

Chris tripped over a pile of saucepans, Susan caught him, and after this they made their way around the house together, Chris hanging on to Susan's arm, Susan and Amanda holding hands,

151

unclasping to sticker anything they wanted. None of them were in the habit of touching other people. All of them—even Amanda, who had lovers—were rather fastidiously inhibited in their ordinary lives. Amanda was prodigal with red stickers. Chris put a yellow one on a Pembroke table that he might use to write on. Susan succumbed to a 1930s Parisian hatbox and a pair of Chinese ivory masks.

—Those masks are nice, Amanda said, jealous. —Clever you, I didn't notice them.

Smitten momentarily with cupidity, Susan wouldn't give them up; she put them in her bag, saving her pleasure in them for exploring later. At the door to Vivien's bedroom, Amanda halted and the others crowded against her, breathing in one another's heat and freshness, aftershave and wool, shampoo: they were middle-aged, but still clean and competent, at least. Here too, everything had been pulled out of drawers and cupboards. All their eyes were drawn to where, beside the single bed with crumpled sheets, no one had cleared away a last cigarette, crushed out slovenly in a jam-jar top. None of them mentioned it. It might have belonged to whoever had made the inventory, but it might also have been Vivien's.

—Do you two have children? Amanda said. —I don't.

Susan's boy and girl were in their twenties; Chris was keen to tell them all about Thea—nine—though he didn't see her often. None of the three, it turned out, currently had a partner.

—I have boyfriends, Amanda explained. —But I live alone, out of choice.

—What's the matter with us? Chris wondered. —None of us have been good at making relationships.

152

Do you think it damaged us, coming here?

Amanda was defensive. —I like my own company.

—Or perhaps we were like that in the first place, and that's why we kept coming.

—Do you remember when we spied on her? Susan said.

—I don't remember spying, said Amanda.

—You must. Isn't it in your diary?

—How do you know about my diary?

—You used to bring it, and read bits out loud to us. You used to write in it while we were watching, telling us you were writing about us, then slamming the book shut if we tried to read it.

Amanda made a false face of contrition. —Did I?

—I took everything too much to heart. That was my problem.

*   *   *

When they were sixteen, seventeen, Vivien still made them tea, and they still ate it, but Mandy was always dieting and Chris and Susan were ravenous, triangles of sandwich making only one mouthful in the new scale of their lives. Torn out of the child bodies that had fitted them purely and exactly, they looked with resentful eyes at Everdene Walk because they couldn't love it again with the same glee. When Vivien enthused over their prospects—university for Chris, modelling for Mandy, for Susan some deep personal adventure—they longed to believe her, but didn't trust that she really knew anything. So they were rude or silent, and knew they disappointed her.

153

Also, they looked at one another differently. They had never met outside the Walk: now they were afraid that they might cross paths in the street or at a disco, and know too much about one another, blowing open the public persona that each so scrupulously controlled. And yet, when Vivien left them alone together, they couldn't resist the luxury of freedom within their exceptional little tribe. Even Susan, in one of her gouts of inhibited awkward eloquence, confessed that there was 'someone' she liked. Mandy told the others what she'd done with boys at parties. She worked to perturb Chris, yet didn't notice when she achieved this. He was delicious at that age, unknown to himself: skinny and jumpy, shadowed lashes dipping on his freckled cheeks, mouth twisted sardonically, a light of wit and nerves playing in his expression. Thirty-five years later, he didn't look so very different, only his qualities, by persisting, had worn out their promise. He was more boyish in his fifties than he had been as a boy.

One summer night, they had told Vivien that they would walk home together; they didn't need a lift. Daddy was old—he hated getting the car out in the evening—and they reassured Vivien that their parents wouldn't worry. Their way was across the Downs, a miles-wide stretch of open grass in the middle of the city, dividing the suburbs from the centre. There was hardly anyone else about. The heady spaces of warm night above and around them made them behave as if they were drunk, swaying and falling into one another, laughing and inventing stories. In the dark, they were unafraid. Mandy seized the others' hands; self-conscious but grateful, they allowed her to tug them close, and swing

154

their arms. It even seemed possible for a moment, as they walked under the shelter of a copse of tall beeches where the grass wasn't cut, that they might do something extraordinary, lie down all three of them in the grass and roll together, kiss together, press together, achieve some kind of interpenetration that all of them were yearning for, though none of them had come anywhere near it (not even Mandy).

Then one of them suggested that they go back and watch Vivien's house. It might have been Susan, because she knew how to get into the den from the public path without going through the Walk; perhaps they all thought that they would be better concealed in the den, for whatever was going to happen next, than under the beeches out in the open. It took a while to get back, and longer to discover which of the dark gardens belonged to No. 33; when eventually they'd struggled over the fence and settled into the little space, they were crowded intimately close together, breathing hard, and their mood changed from the floating blissful playfulness of the Downs to something more intent. The two girls were on either side of Chris, tight against him. They didn't really think they would see anything. They imagined that, after they left, the house was shut up for the night.

A light went on in Vivien's bedroom. The room had French windows and a little balcony, which was not wide enough to sit on but had a continental chic. From the den, they could see right into it. Opening the windows, Vivien leaned her arms on the wrought-iron balustrade, looking out into the night like a heroine in a film. She was wearing a turquoise nightdress under a filmy lacy matching knee-length peignoir: the girls knew that she called it this. With the light behind her, she didn't look bad. Mandy put two fingers in her mouth and wolf-whistled. They expected Vivien to be shocked, to shut the windows hastily. But she only smiled, as if something were amusing, and straightened her back. Then they understood that her moments at the window had been a performance, projected at an imaginary watcher: the whistle had only made him unexpectedly real.

Turning inside, Vivien left the windows open, then came back to set up a folding chair where she had been standing. After a few more minutes she returned again, with a drink, cigarettes and lighter, and a book. She sat, crossed her legs, lit a cigarette, puffed at it in the shallow way she had, and sipped her drink; a slipper with pompoms dangled from her bare foot, which she moved in slow arcs, dipping and pointing the toes whose nails they knew were painted vermilion. Her peignoir fell open at the thigh, nothing unseemly; and, anyway, she had nice legs, for her age. Mandy whistled again, softly; Vivien settled herself more sensuously in her chair, swung her slipper. They dreaded her giving herself away any further, and yet willed her to do so. Chris couldn't wolf-whistle, but he could do fluting whistles like bird calls. While Vivien sat reading for as long as it took her to finish her drink, his bird calls slipped intermittently—swooning, brooding messages—out of the undergrowth, through the warm night. She put down her book, leaned her head back, closed her eyes, sighed, ran her hands luxuriantly down her nightdress. The children couldn't move or speak, in case she heard them; they swallowed with dry throats. They didn't dare look at one another, for fear of spurting out with laughter.

Then at last she stood up and took the chair inside, shutting the window, and the spell that had bound them was broken. Susan got up stiffly, groaning with pins and needles, brushing earth and twigs from her bare knees, whispering that she had to go; she was afraid of what her parents would think if she wasn't back soon. She assured them that she would be fine, making her way across the Downs on her own (and fortunately she was). Chris and Mandy were left alone together.

*   *   *

In the present too, Susan was the first to go. Chris walked out with her to her taxi when it came. They kissed clumsily—he went for two cheeks when she meant to only do one.

—We ought to meet like this again, he said.

—That would be nice.

Susan was insincere, one hand already on the door of her liberating taxi. Her counter-reaction after opening up came faster and more violently, as she aged: she longed to be alone with herself.

—Mandy's right, Chris pursued. —The past's important.

A chill made Susan pull her cardigan tighter; Chris seemed to feel it, too, when his eager look tipped down too far into her strained eyes. Embarrassed, indifferent to him, she burrowed away inside the taxi; its driver, elbow out of the wound-down window, summing Chris up dismissively, put the car in gear. She asked for the station.

Returning inside, Chris wondered aloud to

157

Amanda, who crouched twiddling the knobs of a television with a bulbous green screen, what Susan had thought of him in the old days: it seemed to matter suddenly.

—Wasn't she mad keen on you at one time? In my memory, she as good as told you so. You probably weren't listening. Weren't interested, anyway.

—You're joking.

—It was serious. In so far as they're ever serious, those kiddie crushes.

Chris took this new knowledge in, past the usual apparatus of his ideas and ironies, crowded as a junkyard.

—She did seem haunted. Disappointed. You don't think there'd be any point in me . . .?

—Shouldn't think so. That was a million years ago. It wouldn't be you, haunting her now.

He accepted this, resigned.

But the vibration of passion had been introduced into the darkened room: they both felt it, taken by surprise. They talked about other things: Amanda queried whether books on the shelves, first editions by forgotten novelists, might be worth something. Chris said he doubted it. Meanwhile, he was uncovering more detail in the memory of what had happened between him and Mandy in the den. Not the dream-thing they had all three wanted under the beeches but a twosome more greedily down to earth, his hand pushed under her bra, hers into his unzipped jeans, actually a first for him. Though he hadn't cared for Mandy much, his gratitude had been overwhelming; it had dissolved him. ('Do you like me? Do you like me?' she had kept asking.)

He woke up, for once, to the blossoming of

the present moment. He couldn't make love to Amanda now, in this decomposing house. Could he? They were too old to do it in the garden. Perhaps it didn't matter that she wasn't his type. Anyway, what type was he?

—Aren't you glad I arranged for us to meet? Amanda said, still wanting praise, making her old face of pouting, flirting dissatisfaction.

Susan in her taxi, dusty hatbox on the seat beside her, fingered the ivory masks in her handbag, out of sight: a man and a woman with broad, composed, stylised faces, lowered eyes. She didn't remember them from her childhood. They were meant not for wearing but to hang on a wall, beautiful, carved into the curve of the tusk. She was sure they weren't trash made for tourists. Her smoothing thumb took pleasure in the long cheeks, bulging eyelids, jutting mouths, the ridges of the brows and hair, the woman's earrings and her comb.

She's the One

The winter after her brother killed himself, Ally got a job at a writers' centre near her parents' house, helping out with admin in the office. It wasn't a satisfactory job, only part time and not well paid. She was twenty-two. She had just finished her degree in English literature and should have been building towards some sort of career; she had planned to move to Manchester where she had been at university. But everything like that had had to be put on hold, while at home her family melted down into a kind of madness. It was a relief just to leave the madness behind and drive across the moors four mornings a week to the centre several miles away. She had the use of a car, because for the moment her mum wasn't going to work.

The moors that winter were often under a crust of snow—not enough to blanket them in white but a mean dirty frosting on the hard earth and wilted shrubs. Ally didn't mind the bitter weather. Her guilt at getting out even for a few hours would fall away as she drove, leaving the town behind. Sometimes when she parked at the centre, crunching into the gravelled space between the kitchen and the high black garden wall, where the stones were mossy and ferns grew in the cracks, she was really all right for a moment. I'm really all right, she would think, carefully, lightly, as she pulled the key from the ignition, trying not to examine the sensation too closely or lose it with any sudden movement, as if it were a thin-filmed shiny bubble poised in her chest.

The centre was in a big bleak house built in the

early nineteenth century, isolated in a dip in the middle of the moors beside a river. It had been modernised to suit its new function. A couple of outbuildings along from the kitchen had been converted into a studio for writing workshops and an office, homely with the comfortable ticking of computers and photocopier and fax machine. Fluorescent Post-it notes were stuck to the office shelves, reminding the staff of the things that needed doing, the set procedures for each group of students that came and went. Ally quickly mastered these; she was capable and sensible. The organisers of the centre, Kit and Sam, were pleased to have her helping out. Also, because Ally had always loved reading, the idea was that she would enjoy meeting the writers who taught there—there would be something in it for her, too.

Ally had got the job through the woman her mum had worked for as a secretary, when she was still at work. This woman was a barrister in employment law, and she was on the board of trustees for the centre. In some people, the family's disaster had produced this phenomenon—a crazy energy of organisation on their behalf. Ally was grateful for the job, but it made her mother angry: 'As usual, she comes barging in, thinking she knows best.' Mum was also angry, on the other hand, at their neighbours in the close of ex-council houses, some of whom had been her friends for years but now crept in and out trying to avoid meeting her. Ally appreciated their difficulty. What were they supposed to say, after the first few heartfelt encounters? All ordinary transactions were contaminated: 'How are you?' and 'How's it going?' and 'Nice day.' Even 'Bloody awful day,' which it usually was, would seem to imply an ordinary scale of gloom which her family was far removed from and couldn't possibly yet find a way back to.

* * *

Hilda came to the centre for a week-long fiction-writing course. She was one of those students you learned to pick out at the first encounter as a potential flashpoint, someone who might easily be offended, or offend others; you treated such students with special consideration but kept them at arm's length. She was Canadian, probably in her mid-fifties, small, with thick, perfectly white hair chopped off in a crisp line at her shoulders; she was a vegan, and had requested special dietary arrangements in advance. When everyone gathered around the wood stove in the drawing room of the old house for introductions, Hilda chose to sit cross-legged and straight-backed on the floor, her slight neat body supple like a child's. Although she wasn't unfriendly, Ally noticed that she didn't join in with the others' self-deprecation: a touch of impatience snapped in her expression. Yet she obviously suffered when she had to read out her own work. She must have been good-looking when she was younger, with Scandinavian features, wide mouth and hard cheekbones, something raw in her eyes, their hazel irises flecked with darker brown. She fixed the tutors while they were talking with a steady, critical, attentive gaze.

Although Ally loved books, she had realised since she began working at the centre that she didn't have much interest in knowing how they were written—how characters were developed

162

or plots structured or any of the other things the teachers held forth about and the students soaked up so avidly. All of them, writers and would-be writers, were consumed with a sort of fever over this process of writing and being published; some of the would-bes seemed to hope that by rubbing up close enough against the published ones they might catch something. That week, it was her turn to take the tutors into town for the mid-course lunch. Ann said that she liked Hilda—she'd had an interesting life. But Frank, who was from Glasgow, tall and loose-bodied with a bald patch like a monk's tonsure, complained that she was wearing him down with her persistence.

—She's stuck to my elbow whenever I look down, asking whether I've read her rewrites yet, or what I think of Robertson Davies. She's so intense.

—Intense isn't a bad thing.

—What's her novel about? Ally asked.

—In the sixties, she hung around with arty types in some sort of commune. The central character has an affair with a rock star. It ought to be more interesting. How many Canadian rock stars do you know?

They could think of only Robbie Robertson. They decided that it wasn't him—the character was a singer-songwriter.

—She does this awful folksy thing: he's called the Guitar Player. 'The Guitar Player did this', 'The Guitar Player did that, stuck a spliff under his strings, sent out his lonely song into the night, across the lake.' Imagine writing about a crowd of egomaniacal hippies doing drugs and it's not funny? Also, there's too much nature in it. One tree will do, as far as I'm concerned. Symbolism. One tree can stand in for the whole caboodle.

Some of the writers who came to tutor the courses were nice, but not all of them were. Some were funny about the students, especially the crazies, the ones who brought the two thousand handwritten pages of their novel in a plastic bag, or wrote from the perspective of a donkey abused by its owner. These eccentrics might turn out to be geniuses but usually didn't. Ally wasn't disappointed in the writers: she hadn't expected anything from them in the first place, it hadn't occurred to her to be interested in writers as individuals beyond their work. To her relief no one whose books she'd read ever came to the centre, although sometimes she had to pretend to have read the writers who did. The writers could be fairly crazy, too; you had to be vigilant not to trip up over their vanity and anxiety. Luckily, most of her favourites were dead.

*   *   *

At the end of the course, on her evaluation sheet, Hilda made a number of points about how it could have been better organised. Under the question 'What was the most important thing you learned in your time here?' she left the space empty. A few weeks later Ally stood behind her in a queue at the supermarket. She hadn't realised that Hilda lived nearby but she couldn't have mistaken her, with her crisp white hair, in stretch leggings and trainers and a red down jacket. Ally wasn't working that afternoon. She had told her mum to go to bed and promised to cook tea. In her wire basket she had sausages and eggs and tins of baked beans and a plastic pack of four jam doughnuts, one each (she had another brother, James, fourteen). She'd

164

put on weight since she'd been home; not much, but enough to make her aware of some new soft fat around her waistline and cushioning her chin. Outside it was already dark at four o'clock, a sleety rain was driving across the supermarket car park. In Hilda's basket there was olive oil, a tin of cannellini beans, pasta, a lemon, a bottle of white wine.

Hilda had not noticed Ally waiting behind her, so Ally could easily not have said anything. Seeing the selection of things in Hilda's basket, though— her brave indifference to her surroundings—Ally didn't want her to go off into the night without acknowledgement.

—Hello Hilda, she said. —How's the novel going?

Usually it was the one question that couldn't fail with course-goers. But Hilda turned from the checkout with a face of pure resentment, staring and challenging.

—Who are you? Were you on that course? I don't remember you.

People looked at them. Ally felt exposed, as if she were pretending to be something she wasn't. Almost certainly some of the people looking would know what had happened to her family: it was a small town, and usually she was careful to make herself inconspicuous. Her mother complained that she hid behind her long hair. While Ally explained, admitting that it was unlikely that Hilda would remember her— she'd mostly been in the office, present only once in the evening—Hilda was packing her shopping into the canvas bag she'd brought, deliberately, as if she had a system. She paid with a card, querying something on her bill.

—I thought the olive oil was one-eighty-nine?

—That's only if you buy two bottles, the girl at the

165

till said with flat indifference, not looking up from where she was staring at the slot that would spew the receipt. —If you only buy one, it's two-nineteen. It's a special offer.

—That isn't made very clear on the labelling on the shelf.

Ally was aware that everything about Hilda, especially her ringing, reasonable, confident Canadian voice, was making the till girl resent and despise her.

—I'm sorry I didn't recognise you, Hilda said to Ally, but not warmly, when she was finished. She hiked the canvas bag on to her shoulder. —I'm in a hurry, anyway. I have to go.

—It's OK, don't worry.

The till girl extended the same hostility to Ally: she had been outed now as belonging to Hilda's type, cooking with olive oil, betraying themselves in oblivious loud voices. Even the most minor setbacks, in those months, could throw Ally completely. When she left the supermarket, Hilda was waiting for her where the positive neon universe of shopping bordered on the smudged antimatter outside, cars plashing out of the car park through the wet.

—Shit, that was rude of me, Hilda said. —What's your name?

—Ally. No, really, it's all right.

—Hey, you're upset. I wasn't that bad, was I? I think I owe you an explanation.

—There's other stuff. It's just been a bad day.

—You asked about my novel, that's the thing. I'd waited a lot of years to write that novel. But, if you want to know, my novel died.

Ally wiped her face on her coat sleeve. —I'm sorry. Perhaps it isn't really that bad. Maybe if you put it away for a few weeks and looked at it again you'd feel differently about it. I've heard writers at the centre say that.

—No, really, take it from me, the novel died. What other stuff? What kind of bad day? Can I share? Can I give you a lift somewhere?

Share? Ally thought. No, I don't think so.

She said that she lived only ten minutes' walk away, but Hilda insisted on driving her there—it was on her way—and it was easier to accept than to resist. The car was tiny, continental-looking, green-coloured with a lighter green leaf stencilled on the door, as distinctively alien in the car park as Hilda had been among the shoppers inside. The interior smelled of dog, although there wasn't one: Hilda explained that she had been at work all afternoon—she was a part-time receptionist at the health centre—and she'd had to leave her dog at home.

—Drop me here, please, Ally said. —This is the end of my street. There's no point in turning up into it—you'd only get stuck in the one-way.

Hilda pulled out of the stream of traffic on to the pavement. It was home time, there were queues at the lights going out of town. Ally's parents' house was on an estate at the town's edge; ahead, she could just make out the black slopes of the moors. In the car it was stuffy and slightly disgustingly cosy, the wipers going, the windows steaming up.

—So what was the other stuff? Hilda asked with the engine still running.

Ally, with her hand on the lever, about to open the car door, was thinking that nothing on earth was strong enough to pull this ugly secret out of her, least of all a woman who thought it mattered if her stupid novel had died. She was clenched up with the same

167

resentment as the till girl, at Hilda's ready wisdom shining about like a searchlight, the clean straight-backed way she sat at the steering wheel, her bag full of food for the wrong climate. The next moment, without even knowing that she'd changed her mind, she spilled over with her story—not the full version with all the details, but enough—surprising herself, as if she'd opened her mouth for something quite different.

—*Je-sus*, Hilda said.

It was a relief to have told her. That would teach her not to ask. Ally watched the wipers push the water about in fan shapes on the windscreen.

—I can't just drop you off on the side of the road after you've told me that. Can't I come in? Won't you come home with me? I've got dinner for two. We could talk.

—I have to go. My mum's waiting. I promised I'd make the tea. And I don't need to talk.

—OK, understood. But listen. Will you give me your phone number? I'd love to call. May I? We'll fix up something. Come and meet the dog.

Only to be free of her, Ally wrote the number on an envelope that Hilda found in her bag. That'll be the last I hear from her, she thought.

—Your name's Ally, right? Hilda checked, leaning across the front seat after her.

*   *   *

Ally read novels, wrapped up in her duvet beside the radiator in her bedroom, borrowing them from the centre and the public library, sometimes finishing one and starting another without even changing her position or getting up to make coffee, like an addict.

She knew that this wasn't the right kind of reading. Studying for her literature degree, she had learned how to analyse the words and the themes, she had worked dutifully on her essay style, imitating academic articles. She imagined the reading she did now as like climbing inside one of those deep old beds she'd seen in a museum, with a sliding door to close behind you: even as she was suffering with a book and could hardly bear it, felt as if her heart would crack with emotion or with outrage at injustice, the act of reading it enclosed and saved her. Sometimes when she moved back out of the book and into her own life, just for a moment she could see her circumstances with a new interest and clarity, as if they belonged to someone else.

It was around this time that Ally's mum started wearing Ryan's shirts under her clothes. The first time Ally caught her doing it, she arrived home early one lunchtime and when she came in the back door Mum looked up with a guilty face from washing dishes at the sink. Through all those weeks, their house had never lapsed from its perfect tidiness and order. Last thing at night, her parents still rinsed out the coffee cups, plumped up the cushions on the sofa, unplugged the television. Her mother picked up threads from the carpet and put them in the waste-paper basket. Ally knew right away when she came into the kitchen that something was wrong in her mother's shape, something bulky and distorting, when usually she was petite and trim. Ryan hadn't been enormous for an eighteen-year-old but on his mother his checked lumberjack shirt was swamping, enveloping. Her thin neck looked scrawny, poking out through the top of it; her neat faded face without its make-up seemed scoured clean. She hadn't pulled the collar of the shirt out over the neck of her sweatshirt, as if she were hoping that no one would notice it, but it stuck up anyway.

—What are you doing wearing that thing?

She shouldn't have said anything, but she couldn't help it. Swapping clothes was the kind of thing that Ryan had done with his girlfriend Yvonne. Yvonne would come downstairs after the two of them had been shut up for hours in his bedroom, pink-faced, wearing one of Ryan's tops, pulling the too-long sleeves down over her hands, flaunting to the world this outward sign of her feminine smallness snuggled against his bulk. When Mum bought Ryan a perfectly good pair of black Thinsulate gloves, he exchanged them for some silly cheap spangly ones of Yvonne's. No one in the family had exactly objected to this at the time, but there was no doubt that they'd thought it soppy. They'd teased Ryan for being sentimental—he was like their dad, still moony over Mum after all these years. Mum in particular didn't have much time for Yvonne. Now she was wearing his shirt herself, and it was a sign of how far she had been broken down.

—It makes me feel better if I can smell him.

Ally wrapped her arms around her from behind. She pressed her face into her neck, sniffing the shirt collar. Her mum held herself stiffly apart inside the embrace.

—It doesn't smell of anything except fabric softener.

—Underneath it I can smell him.

Ally willed herself to remember real things about her brother, neutral things, uncontaminated by the new aura, like worship and dread, that was attached to the idea of him. She remembered that after he'd

170

finished his A2 exams in the summer, for example, when he was supposed to be looking for a job, he had played his Nintendo Wii in the afternoons, downstairs in the sitting room in the boxers and T-shirt and socks he had slept in, Ally protesting at the sight of his thickly hairy legs. Her mother wouldn't have wanted to wrap herself in the smell of him then. Ally longed to climb back inside the safety of that time, when none of them wanted too much of one another.

* * *

There had been some tormented to-and-fro between the two families, Ryan's and Yvonne's, telephone calls and visits, breakdowns and comfortings, an evening when Yvonne's mother called Ally's mum, begging her to talk to Yvonne because she was threatening to do what Ryan had done 'since everyone blamed her for it anyway'. Yvonne was one of those miniature girls teenage boys love: their smallness seems to promise that they will be sweetly malleable. She had a mass of curls the colour of ripe wheat, tight golden skin, a child's body so pliant that she could still do cartwheels and backflips. She wrote all over her hard tiny hands with ballpoint pen: telephone numbers, silly faces that changed their expression when she moved her fingers. But actually Yvonne wasn't malleable—she was steely. She'd had Ryan running around after her whims as if she were a princess. — She might as well enjoy it, Ally's mum had said back then. —She'll be a dowdy little cow by the time she's thirty.

The awful intimacy between the two families subsided after the first weeks. They drew apart; they couldn't speak to one another any more. In those sessions they had dragged too deep, dredging up some rotten taste from the bottom of their lives which tainted all their interactions afterwards. Then Yvonne began texting Ally, and lying in wait for James on his way home from school. Even James knew not to tell Mum about this. Yvonne claimed that she only wanted advice on what she should do with the stuff that Ryan had given her; she made James take a plastic bag full of his CDs. —Chuck it all out, Ally texted back. —If you don't want it.

At the inquest it all came out about the letter that Ryan had left, with messages for Yvonne—how amazing she was, how his life wasn't worth living without her. In the context these seemed less like loving compliments than like punishments. Ally could imagine how it must feel to have these ideas stuck to you, impossible to clean off. But she couldn't make herself like Yvonne any better.

*   *   *

Hilda rang her.

—Ally? Is that Ally? Remember me? I was the bitch in the supermarket. You're having a hell of a time. Why don't you come out here and yell about it?

Ally felt remote from anyone who talked like this. But her mum encouraged her to get out, make a new friend. Most of the girls Ally had known at school had moved away from home, to go to university or to find jobs. She'd had a boyfriend in Manchester, but that relationship had melted away in the fierce assault of the first days of crisis. She hadn't wanted him anywhere near it.

—She's not exactly a friend, Mum. She's older

172

than you.

—Well, someone you can talk to. It's not good for you, being stuck here all the time with us. At least James has got school.

—I don't know why everyone thinks I need to talk.

She called in at Hilda's one afternoon, after she had finished work at the centre. The cottage wasn't where she'd thought it was. She had to drive around for a while before she found it, at the top of a hill a mile outside Kirby, with a stand of woods beyond it. Hilda in her red down jacket came out with the dog as she parked: it was a short-haired terrier, alert and intelligent, white with a brown patch over one eye. Hilda proposed that they take a walk right away, before it got dark. Ally hadn't imagined them walking. She was wearing her pink trainers, and had to borrow wellingtons from Hilda. They followed a path invisible under the snow, down towards the woods along the side of a big L-shaped field, the dog scouting ahead of them, racing back on her tracks to herd her humans together, straining her ears yearningly at the perturbed, watchful sheep. The afternoon was still and soundless, frozen. There had been a fresh fall of snow the night before, and the fences and trees stood out black against it. Already the moon had risen, a flake of waxy alabaster in a blue sky thin with light.

Hilda complained about the farmer whose land they were walking on. She said that she had contacted the RSPCA because he didn't treat the foot rot in his sheep, and that he'd tried to stop her walking there although it was a public right of way. It was true that quite a few of the sheep seemed to be hobbling on three legs, or half kneeling, their front legs bent at the joint. Ally worried that the farmer would come out to

173

confront them. She didn't want to have to take sides. As she tramped beside Hilda on the way back, the day draining out of the sky seemed to empty her, too, leaving her weightless. When they arrived back at the cottage they could still see each other clearly, but the light was at its moment of transition, and as soon as they went inside the night outside the windows appeared perfectly dark. In the cottage downstairs there was only one room, with a kitchen at one end and a sitting room at the other, a flagged floor and a wood fire smouldering in a wide stone hearth, one wall stripped back to the naked stone. Hilda put logs on the fire and switched on a couple of lamps.

The room was uncluttered, considering how small it was, but everything in it was striking and eccentric: the faded rugs, the pictures on the walls, a wool blanket woven in bright colours flung over the back of the sofa, collections of stones and twisted weathered deadwood from the moors. The effect seemed spontaneous, but Ally knew that it must have taken a huge effort to get it to this state, removing all the layers of paint and wallpaper and carpeting and cosiness. There were photographs of Hilda's three grown children, two daughters and a son. Hilda said that she had divorced her husband twenty years ago and had mostly brought up the children by herself. He was an Englishman. The only good thing he'd ever done for her was introduce her to this part of the country. She'd lived in Leeds for years, had moved out to the cottage when her younger daughter left home. Then she'd saved and bought herself a whole year off work, to get on with her novel. When she abandoned the novel and the money ran out, she'd decided to get a local job, part time.

—I can manage, she said. —Cut the consumer

crap. We don't need half as much as they want to persuade us to buy. How long I'll stay at the health centre I don't know. The staff aren't friendly.

Ally couldn't imagine Hilda fitting in around here. People would think she was too full of herself: her neat frame seemed packed up tight with personality and experience. Her self-sufficiency made Ally feel unformed. She hung on to the mean little nugget of knowledge: that the writers on the course had said Hilda was too intense, had no sense of humour. There was no sign of a television anywhere in the cottage, only shelves of books.

—Didn't you ever want to go home to Canada?

—England's home. I've lived here longer now than I lived there. Anyway, two of my children live in London, and one's in Dundee. I couldn't live thousands of miles away from them.

Hilda told Ally to wrap herself in the blanket in front of the fire: she explained that it was a button blanket, made by a Tlingit artist. Then she brought her tea and a slab of apple cake she'd made herself, without eggs or dairy.

—I want to ask you how you are, she said, sitting on a cushion on the hearthrug. —Real question, not the polite version. You can tell me it's none of my business. We hardly know each other.

—I'm OK.

—You honoured me with your confidence the other day.

—I'm really OK. Why don't you tell me about your novel instead? You said you had been waiting all your life to write it.

She thought that Hilda flinched. —Outside the shop? Did I say that?

—Something like that.

175

Hilda considered carefully. —You're angry because I talked about it so seriously, as if my novel were a disaster in the real world. But of course it can't be weighed in that world. Against the life of one of my children, say, it isn't a feather. Or against the life of anyone's child.

—It mattered to you, though.

Ally wasn't interested in the novel itself. She wanted to dig down to the raw shame of this failure in Hilda, this thing inside her poisoning everything, cut off and spoiled and shrivelled up.

Hilda told her the story of the Guitar Player. In the late sixties, when Hilda was fifteen, her mother had had an affair with a singer-songwriter. It had happened in a big house on a lake in north-western Ontario, where Hilda's mother was employed as a live-in cook and cleaner. The house had belonged to a Toronto music producer, who brought his friends out to party in the summer. Even while the affair was happening, Hilda's mother had gone on cleaning and washing up and cooking. She said she'd rather be busy than hang around doing nothing. She refused to take any money beyond her wages. She really was the kind of woman that folk singers sang about in those days, or she made herself into that kind of woman: good at growing things and cooking and healing and comforting. That summer, Hilda's mother had gone around barefoot and worn long dresses, with her hair down to her waist, and the guests had treated her as if she were a kind of child of nature because she lived out by the lake all year round. All of them had been a bit in love with her, especially after the Guitar Player had chosen her. She hadn't tried to explain to these guests the complications of her real life on the lake.

At the end of the summer, the Guitar Player had moved on and Hilda's mother had never seen him again, but he'd had a success with a song that she always believed was about her: 'She's the One', a hymn to beauty that could also be interpreted as a message of farewell or apology. Hilda's mother had bought the album and learned all the words. And after she married Hilda's stepfather, whenever they had rows she would retreat to her den and play it over and over, singing along. By that time she'd cut her hair and was working as a receptionist at one of the lake hotels. But Hilda knew that the song wasn't really about her mother, although she had never told her so. She knew this because those words—'She's the one'—were what the Guitar Player had said to Hilda when he came looking for her for the first time. She'd slept in the attic of the big house: at night she used to stand on a chair, craning her head out of the skylight to watch the grown-ups drinking and partying in the garden below or undressing to go skinny-dipping in the lake. When the Guitar Player had come into Hilda's room and lifted the sheet on her bed, he'd said not 'You're the one' but 'She's the one', as if he were describing her to somebody else, some objective judge watching.

She had been afraid, of course, but not sorry, not at the time. He was as moody and skinny as a boy, but he had a power that drew all the yearning in the place towards him, including hers. He'd hardly spoken to her before that, but he must have noticed her watching him. His real presence in her room had seemed a kind of miracle, refracted and thickened through everyone's adulation of him, through his pictures in magazines and on album covers. He'd been pretty high that night, exalted and weird; there were a lot of drugs around that summer. He'd said all kinds of strange things—Hilda was surprised that he could remember any of it afterwards, but quite a lot of it had found its way into the song.

*   *   *

Hilda told her the real name of the singer-songwriter and Ally didn't recognise it. A crumb of apple cake had stuck to Hilda's cheek as she talked. She was at that tipping point in middle age. Mostly she was animated, buoyant, and flexible, her skin was good, and in spite of her white hair she seemed to belong to the world of choice and strength. Then in some trick of the light, or because she sagged her chin into her wrinkling neck, or her too-short trousers rode up above her ankle socks as she was sitting cross-legged, Ally saw for a moment the old woman she would become, vulnerable and stubborn, cut adrift. Ally knew about the sixties—hippies and psychedelia and free love—but they seemed actually less real to her than Victorian times. If Hilda had said that she'd seen Catherine Earnshaw's ghost tapping at the window, it would have had more of a thrill of possibility.

—It was a kind of rape. It was child abuse. But that wasn't how I saw it at the time. Later, in the seventies, I got very angry about it.

—What d'you think about it now?

—When I was trying to write the novel, I made such an effort to remember it exactly. I played all the old music. Of course, it can't mean anything to you. How could I convey the power of those people? That was it, that

178

was my failure—I couldn't convey it. But it was real. It happened. It was almost a physical thing—you couldn't separate out the music and the giftedness and the youth. There was like a hum of sex in the air all the time.

Ally made an effort to imagine Hilda as a fifteen-year-old, but even the room they were in made this difficult. Its uncompromising style conveyed the whole long adult effort of putting a life together. Hilda said that, in her twenties, the story of what had happened had blocked her; for years she hadn't been able to get past the cheat or the promise of it. She hadn't told anyone about it, certainly not her mother, not even her husband. She'd saved it up. She'd told herself that one day she would put it in a book, not to make a scandal—as if anyone would care!—but just to be finally free of it. And once she'd begun to think of it as a story it had stopped troubling her; the idea of writing it had even come to be a comfort to her in bad times, a resource stored inside her, opening possibilities in the future.

—But it was a dud, she said. —It was a wrong idea. I couldn't do it. What I wanted to say died on me. It died inside.

*   *   *

Hilda gave Ally a key to the cottage.

—You can come here any time, if you need space. Make yourself a fire if I'm not here. Grab what you like to eat. Tilly will love to see you—she hates to be locked up in the house alone.

Ally took the key, but couldn't imagine that she'd ever need it. Then one afternoon when things were bad at home—trouble was blowing up around

179

James's refusing to go to school—she drove to the cottage and let herself in. She told her mother that she was walking Hilda's dog, as a favour. She did take Tilly out, and then when they got back she made a fire and wrapped herself in the blanket and picked out one of the books from Hilda's shelves, losing herself in it so completely and deeply that when Hilda came back from work, pushing open the door, Ally looked up startled and didn't know for a moment where she was. After that, she started calling in at the cottage once or twice a week; sometimes Hilda was home and sometimes Ally was alone there. When Hilda went to Dundee for the weekend, to stay with her daughter who had cats, Ally slept at the cottage overnight, keeping Tilly company.

One evening when she and Hilda were sharing a bottle of red wine, she explained what Ryan had done to kill himself, hanging himself on the stairs using a length of spare washing line. She'd never had to tell anyone this before: either they knew already or they didn't like to ask, but Hilda had come straight out with it. They were sitting staring at each other from opposite ends of the sofa, with their legs tucked under them; the dog in her basket was panting with pleasure in the warmth of the fire.

—Mum would have found him, Ally said. — Usually she gets home twenty minutes before my dad, except that day on an impulse she went the roundabout way to buy vegetables at the farm shop. I was away in Manchester. My other brother had football after school. It wouldn't have made any difference to what happened—there was no chance of stopping him or anything. He had died already, hours before. But it meant that Mum didn't have to find him. Dad found him instead. Dad said that that

180

was the only saving grace in the whole thing, her buying those vegetables.

The wine made little waves in her glass, in time with the pounding of her heart. Hilda reached over to pull the blanket up around Ally's shoulders.

—Did you have any idea that he was so depressed?

—Now when we go over the music he was playing, and what he put on Facebook, everything suggests it. At the time we just thought he was going through a phase. In fact he was just going through a phase. Only, stupid moron, he didn't leave himself any chance to come out of it.

—It's a terrible thing for his girlfriend, Hilda sighed. —It really fucks her up.

Ally couldn't bear the idea that Hilda would imagine Yvonne as something she wasn't, some kind of tragic heroine. —They were always splitting up and getting back together again, working themselves up into a lather of feeling, one way or another. It didn't mean anything.

—But that's what you think love's all about when you're a kid.

—That kind of love makes me sick. It's such a fake.

When Hilda came back from Dundee she brought Ally a stone she'd picked up on a beach there, oval and flat and black, striped with pinkish crystal. — Pounded by the North Sea, she said. In Hilda's house it was a beautiful thing, but it only looked odd among the ornaments on her bedroom shelf at home, as if a piece of outdoors had got indoors by mistake.

*   *   *

One morning when Ally was at the writing centre,

181

double-checking the details of next year's programme of courses before they sent it off to press, Yvonne turned up, hovering outside the office door. Ally recognised her through the glass before she saw Ally inside: it was a fine day, brilliantly cold, so that blue sky was patched in the frame of the door behind Yvonne's yellow hair and short white bomber jacket. Her shoulders were hunched with the cold, her skinny midriff bare, hardly bulging over the top of tight jeans. She put her face up close to the glass, peering in. Ally felt like a fish in a bowl, helpless to escape being seen.

—I have to talk to you, Yvonne said once she'd got the door open, looking around suspiciously and showing no sign of wanting to cross the threshold of the office.

No 'please' or 'if you're not busy'.

Ally took down her coat and suggested they walk along the river. She left a note on the desk for Kit. It was the second day of a short-story course, and all the students were on the loose outdoors with notebooks and pens. They must have been given some writing exercise. Everywhere you looked, one of them seemed to be staring at nothing, drinking it in, transfixed: a dead stalk of dock weed or the blank corner of a stone wall or an icicle dribbled from the lip of a gutter. Dedicatedly they scribbled in their notebooks, squinting at the nothing from all angles.

—Shit a brick, muttered Yvonne, keeping her eyes on the ground. —What are they supposed to be doing?

Ally felt bound to apologise for the centre. She said that they were practising observational skills.

—Observing my arse, Yvonne said.

Her thin little face which had used to look creamy, was peaky, blue around the lips. Ally had always guessed that underneath Yvonne's neat sweetness—plucked straight brows, small nose, pink ears—something ferrety was waiting to appear. Yvonne walked rolling on her heels with her arms wrapped across her chest, hands tucked up into her jacket sleeves for warmth. The path dropped to the river and she looked around her, not enthusiastically, as if she didn't often find herself in the country. Bare alders and ash and blackthorn made a twiggy haze against the sun, which was already close to dropping behind the steep side of the river valley; the cold tea-brown water coiled thickly in its bed. Ally felt better once they were past the last of the writers.

—Everybody hates me, Yvonne said. —I suppose that's what he wanted.

—We've been over all this, said Ally. —Nobody hates you.

Yvonne fished for something in her tight jeans pocket, thrust it out closed in her fist. —I wanted to give you this back.

Ally put her hands behind her. —I don't want it. What is it?

—A stupid ring Ryan gave me.

—I don't want it.

In a spasm of temper Yvonne swung around and opened her hand, flinging away into the river something tiny that gave out one glint of light before it was swallowed without a splash, the water healing instantly behind it. The moment she'd done it she shrieked, pressing her hands across her mouth, and said that she hadn't meant to let it go, it was an accident.

—Ally, help me get it back!

—Don't be silly. The water's too deep. You couldn't find it in a million years. It doesn't matter.

Yvonne went on shrieking and pleading. Crouching on the path she started untying her trainers, dragging and clawing at the laces as if she were going to wade in. On an impulse, because the whole scene disgusted her, Ally found herself calmly stepping into the river with her trainers still on, wading across the large flat submerged stones at its edge. At first she hardly felt the cold, only the pull of the moving water as if something were clamped around her ankles. Then she stepped down into a deeper channel, among the smaller toffee-coloured pebbles of the river bed; the water here was halfway up to her calves, then up to her knees, soaking her trousers, wrapping them against her legs, snatching her breath away with the shock of the cold. The force of the current where the river ran faster almost knocked her off balance, though it looked lazy on the surface. She steadied herself by hanging on to a slippery boulder sticking up midstream and wondered if she should go any farther. Her jaw was clenched. It was difficult to remember how to move her feet in the trainers that began to feel numbingly huge and heavy.

She didn't care about the ring: she had stepped into the water only to make a point against the hysterical performance on the riverbank, to show it up in some way that was deliberate and disdainful. When she turned to look back at Yvonne, she was surprised at how far she had come: Yvonne on the path seemed distant, hugging her elbows, shouting directions that Ally couldn't hear over the water rushing past. It seemed a different universe out here in the river. The whole scene, the sad story that had brought them together, was framed for her for a moment as if from some far-off future perspective, and her rage against Yvonne washed out of her. Wanting only to be kind, she began hunting for the ring in all seriousness, peering at the river bed, fishing for gleams in the water, her hands aching from the cold as if the flesh were being dragged off her bones. She realised that Yvonne was shouting from the bank for her to come back, please come back. It didn't matter, Yvonne shouted. It was only a ring.

At that moment Ally saw it, caught just underwater in a crevice in a jagged chunk of shale, its gold picked out where a beam of the late light slanted at an angle from the water's surface. She put out her hand to take it. And when she had it safe in her clenched fingers, she waded with some difficulty back to where Yvonne was reaching out for her. (—You stupid mad fuck, Yvonne stormed. —What did you think you were doing?) She didn't drown.

In the Cave

After the sex, he fell asleep. That wasn't what Linda had expected. Cheated—returned too soon into her own possession—she lay pinned for a while under his flung arm, looking into the corners of the high ceiling where purple shadows bloomed and a flossy strand of cobweb kept time in a draught she couldn't feel. She liked his flat, what she'd seen of it, better than her own. Books were piled everywhere on the floor, a tide of curiosities was flooded through the rooms in disorder: bird skulls, netsuke, fossils, Christmas cracker jokes pinned on a noticeboard, little animated toys his children had made (he was divorced with two teenage boys), postcard Hammershoi, a marimba, an original nineteenth-century tin zoetrope—an early machine for making moving pictures. (He'd shown her how it worked, she'd been afraid then in case they were carried past the moment when something other than companionable chat was possible.) Photographs of cave paintings everywhere. Her own home was too poky and timid and smothered with tending. And where did he have the money from, to rent a flat in Bloomsbury? (She was in Tottenham.)

But she wasn't in love, though she had been ready to be. Love sank down gently from where it had been swollen in expectation—she imagined a red balloon deflating to a foolish remnant. Lightly, he snored. He was jet-lagged, he'd flown back only yesterday from South Africa. Politely, she eased from underneath his weight. There was only this substantial moment really, for all the sticky trickle

186

on her thighs, and their bodies' forms and smells imprinted recently and urgently upon each other: of mutually uncomprehending encounter. She didn't dislike his body, although she had been two inches taller than he was when they were standing up. He was compact, commanding, energetic; careless of his appearance, balding, with a remainder of fine auburn hair. His spirit was in his blue prominent eyes; now they were closed, lids flickering with dream-life, she was released to perceive him with detachment.

What was she doing here? Mockery sprang up savagely again from where she had suppressed it after they met and got on so well (first time Ozu at the BFI, second time dinner at a French place in Hornsea High Street, third time lucky)—at herself, for having advertised, which she'd never thought she'd do. Now she drowned in shame at the idea of the sprightly words she'd used in her own description, so wincingly anxiously calculated to lead to just this moment.

Oh well never mind.

The sheet was twisted into a rope underneath her—that clean sheet badly tucked in, and the clean duvet and pillowcases, had let her know he too had been planning, when he suggested she come round for early supper at his place. He had advertised too. Now, careful not to wake him, she got up out of bed, wrapping herself in his cotton throw although she wasn't really afraid of his seeing her. Her body was all right, still straight and slender; it was in your face and hands that your age showed first, and you couldn't hide those away. Still, she was out of practice; it might be rash to parade around naked as if she thought she was twenty. The bathroom light wasn't consoling, when she shut the door behind her and turned it on. She avoided her own eyes, and used his flannel—why not? since he'd been in there—to wash between her legs.

When she came out again he hadn't moved from where he lay face down in the bed. She couldn't help feeling sidelined; as if this oblivion was what he'd desired and she'd been merely the passage through to it. Her clothes were dropped on the floor where he and she had stood fumbling together, taking them off; recovering them, Linda carried them through into the living room where they had eaten (something nice but faintly risky, indigestible, squid-ink pasta with mussels and cream), sitting side by side on the sagging chaise longue because the table was impossibly heaped up with iMac and papers. It was dark now—it must be almost ten o'clock. She put on the sequence of garments chosen in such anticipation for taking off, comical as running a wedding video backwards. At first while she was dressing, she thought that she would let herself right away out of the flat, take the Tube home, leave him a note. They might meet up again, or they might not. Her heart wouldn't break, she was safe, its muscle toughened after the years of accumulations from two long relationships, one short marriage (no children).

When they removed to the bedroom they had left IKEA lamps switched on behind them; by their light now Linda, lingering, dressed but in bare feet so that she made no noise, sandals looped across a finger, bag on her shoulder, moved about his room in his absence as if she was moving inside the shape of his mind. She found on the shelves books that he'd written, quite a few, with decent academic publishers. So, he must be fairly successful in his field; though she knew, because he'd told her, that

188

he worked to some extent in the shadow of one of the big innovative thinkers, following up the Professor's hunches with his meticulous research. Perhaps he got serious grants for his fieldwork studying North American and Australian rock art. Perhaps the Bloomsbury flat was part of some fellowship deal.

He had talked a lot about his work; but he had seemed to be interested in hers, too—she was an art therapist, working with clients with mental health problems. They had seemed, over the dinner in Hornsea six weeks ago, to have so much in common. She had built up a whole tall, hopeful, dreamy, precarious edifice out of their common ground while he was away, in defiance of her usual fatalism; she had invented some convenient simulacrum of him, as it seemed to her now—a twin for herself, to fit her need. Luckily, out of some good instinct of self-preservation, she hadn't announced her happiness to anyone among her friends.

It wasn't the sex that had spoiled it.

Something had happened—a drop in her hopes— just before she made the move that saved them from the zoetrope; he had spun its tin drum for her, so that the tiny horses circled in their endless wave of movement, legs clenching and then releasing, kicked back behind. Now, afterwards, while he slept and she was left alone, there was time to think. She fingered through the recollections for whatever was concealed at their centre, little nub of ice. Cold, getting colder, coldest—there!

Was that all? Such a slight thing, in passing.

She had been so moved, thinking of his life's work. In the restaurant the rich smells of

189

meat and wine had seemed to suffuse what he described; visionary animals looming out of torchlit darkness. He had been lucky, he said, getting special permission to have his twenty permitted minutes in the caves at Lascaux; they were closed to visitors now, after the discovery of micro-organisms growing in there, caused by the presence of too many people. He had told her that the latest thinking, based partly on the practices of contemporary hunter-gatherer societies, was that the paintings may have been the product of induced shamanistic hallucinations, projected on to the rock and marked out there. And he had said that for the people who painted Lascaux, the rock face may have seemed only a skin stretched between them and another order of reality. For all those weeks he was absent in South Africa, these possibilities had seemed to have some kind of promise for her. She had spoken about the cave paintings to the clients she worked with in her art classes; some of them were susceptible to visions. Sharing his ideas around, she felt the same secret excitement as when she was a teenager, weaving certain names into her conversation.

And then this evening, as she crouched in front of the zoetrope, peeking through its slot while he spun it for her, he'd explained its trick. His voice had had a giggle in it, of boyish pleasure at debunking sentimentalities.

—It's like the hallucinations the cave painters saw. You can reproduce those visions in laboratory conditions. It's just neurons firing, telling you something's happening when it isn't. I'm not a neurobiologist, but it's something to do with the causal operator, interconnections between the

190

frontal and inferior parietal lobes. Makes you feel you're in the presence of something other: the ineffable. When you aren't. There is no ineffable. It's just a trick of your own mind, deluding itself.

Linda hadn't protested —but isn't there another order of reality? What was the point? Who wanted to appear sentimental?

How small. Just that. One of those tiny twitches in conversation that, unbeknownst to the speaker, tear fissures in the moment, out of which power and pleasure drain. How disappointing. She had seen then that he had his trouser belt pulled tight at a point too high up on his waist, as middle-aged men do; it made her vulnerable, noticing. The bones dried out, the sinews hardened. He had told her in the restaurant that after they closed Lascaux they'd built a replica of parts of the original cave for visitors to enjoy; imagining a plaster rock face, electric torchlight, ersatz exclamations, she had said she'd rather not see it at all. When she was younger, she had not been vain, but had trusted her appearance to be quietly itself, not beautiful: narrow face, coffee-coloured skin, bushy black hair (some Malay in there somewhere, some Portuguese). Nowadays, in the mirror at the centre of the familiar surround of her own dressing-table—pots and bottles, souvenirs, draped scarves and beads—only her face was not unchanging. Mostly she accepted the changes. Occasionally they anguished her, seemed abysmally sad, irrevocable as if a bottle had slipped out of her hand to smash.

Outside the tall uncurtained windows of the flat, trees moved in the square: clotted, massy darkness against purple-lit sky. She ought to go. There was no need to leave a note for him. She didn't want to argue with this man about neurobiology; no one changed their mind, ever, in those kinds of argument. But if she stood there watching the trees for much longer, then he would wake up and wrap himself in the cotton throw, come out to stand in the doorway behind her: everything would be more complicated. Because the arguments themselves were only a skin stretched across darkness. She remembered the horses in the zoetrope, drawing in and throwing out their legs, over and over, in the two opposite impulses, systole and diastole. And how because the movement was unending, she had put out her hand to find him.

Pretending

My friend Roxanne was from the Homes. Roxanne chose me for her friend, I didn't choose her. She had always been on a different table, with the naughty girls: she had been one of the naughtiest. I don't think we'd ever even spoken, until on the day we began Junior Three she put her grubby furry pencil-case on the desk beside mine and sat down there as calmly as if it had been prearranged between us. At first I thought it was a joke, which would end in my humiliation, so I wouldn't look at her. The teacher thought this too, she noticed us uneasily. We were new to her class, but it was a small school, the teachers knew all the children, they knew that girls like Roxanne weren't meant to be friendly with girls like me.

But Roxanne didn't get up to any of her usual tricks. When I put up my desk lid to put my new books inside the desk, she didn't knock it down on my head. Usually when the teacher was talking Roxanne twitched in her seat like a trapped cat, sitting on her hands to keep them from straying, her head twisting around to see what the boys were doing every time there was the sound of a scuffle or a muffled protest. Now she gazed at Mrs Hazlehurst, seeming to soak up every word she was saying. Mrs Hazlehurst was choosing the ink monitor and the milk monitor; she was telling us how hard we had to work, if we wanted to pass in two years' time the examinations for free places in the grammar schools. Roxanne volunteered for everything, holding her arm up straight above her head and tensed and still, although she wasn't chosen. When it came to playtime she gripped on to me as we filed down the corridor to go outside, not painfully but determinedly; she wasn't going to let me go. I was afraid of her and hot at the idea that the others were watching us. I had had a couple of friends in Junior Two and of course they would have expected us to go on sitting and playing together, although our friendship hadn't been passionate. As Roxanne marched me past them they seemed already faint and pale, as if they belonged to the weak past.

—What do you play? Roxanne demanded.

—I dunno. Whatever the others are playing.

—That's boring. Come on. We'll think of something else.

The boys' playground was on the left and the girls' on the right; they were deep concreted pits between very high stone walls. The girls' playground extended on one side into a covered area underneath the school building, supported on iron pillars; we called this the shed, and when it rained it was our shelter. Roxanne led the way in here, still hanging on to me as if she was afraid I might run. It was an eerie echoing space, almost dark at its far end where the big bins were and the padlocked grey-painted doors into the boiler room and the room where the caretaker kept the broken desks and blackboards. We sat down on the low wall in front of the bins. Everyone outside was still standing around in awkward groups, not sure how to begin yet in the new hierarchy, with a new top class and new Junior Ones arrived from the infant school. Roxanne was inches shorter than me; I was tall, and clumsy with what my mother called puppy fat. I also had two big white front teeth like

194

spades, which I had hated ever since they intruded their way into my mouth; I tried not to open it and show them. Roxanne's lithe little brown-skinned body made the boys call her a tomboy, although close up to her I realised that this wasn't right, she didn't have the boys' animal carelessness, she was too intently conscious of herself. Her red cotton dress was skimpy over her barrel chest, I could see her quick breathing. The skin of her face was very thin and fine, drawn tight over the bone beneath, and her head was round and neat as a nut: she was one of those children disconcertingly printed with a set of grown-up features, too finished and expressive. Her dark, silky, curly hair was cropped short.

—What do you want to play? she said, turning on me with intensity. —A pretending game. You can be whatever you like.

I shrugged.

—What do you like best? I'm good at making up these games. If you give me an idea, I'll make a game.

—Horses, I said, trying to think of something. —I like horses.

I thought she was going to give up on me. I was a very conventional child, I knew I was. I saw a flicker of exasperation. Horses! Horses didn't mean anything to her. They didn't really mean much to me either; I had read some pony books, that was all. With an effort that was almost a visible shudder she pulled herself back on track.

—Horses, she said. —All right. We'll try that.

She closed her eyes. The life of her eyes was extinguished for a moment but through their lids I could still see her thoughts darting. When she opened them again they were full of resolution.

195

—All right. Pretend we're horses. Wild ones. Take your hairband off. You have to shake your mane like this. There's a wicked farmer who's trying to catch us and sell us. We have to reach the island where we'll be safe from him, but there's a dangerous river we have to cross to get to it.

She jumped to her feet then and snickered and tossed her head and stamped her foot. She seemed to me miraculously horse-like. I took my hairband off and put it safe in my pocket, then we galloped around the playground, pawing and whinnying, throwing back our heads and shaking our hair; when we spoke we changed our ordinary voices into a kind of breathy neighing. At first I felt like an idiot and I only did it because I didn't dare disobey Roxanne, who had thought up the game especially for me. I saw my old friends watching, from the sidelines as usual. The others had started playing their own things, which some of the popular Junior Four girls were organising. These popular girls weren't used to the sight of Roxanne and me together, they stared and whispered, drooping their arms round one another's necks, which was a thing I hated. I thought they were like witches when they hung together like that, as if they only had one body, all thinking the same thoughts, always disapproving of something. A teacher had read us a story once about some old witches who shared one eye, taking turns to clap it into their foreheads. After a few minutes of the horse game, I began to forget about everybody. I didn't exactly stop knowing that we were in the real playground, pretending something, but a different life welled up from inside me and took possession of my body, so that I could feel the romance of horse-being overwhelming my prosaic self.

—I don't think I can go any further, I neighed when we came to the edge of the river (which ran past the door to the girls' toilet block). —I feel too weak.

—Fear not, young colt, said Roxanne.

She would always surprise me by knowing the right words for whatever we played, like using 'mane' and 'colt', even though she wasn't interested in horses. I had imagined that the children from the Homes, because they had to wear hand-me-down clothes and were looked after by women they called their 'Aunties', would be somehow deprived of these kinds of knowledge. Then she invented an extraordinary movement for horses swimming, holding back her head on her neck, making a nervous big digging movement with her hands, lifting her knees; and it was as if I could see them, the beautiful band of noble beasts giving themselves up courageously to the swift-flowing treacherous river, holding up their fine heads out of the current. After a hiatus midstream when I was in danger of being swept away, and Roxanne, swimming by my side, saved me, nudged me onwards with her nose, we both struggled out on the far bank, shaking ourselves dry, safe at last.

—See-ee-ee? she neighed. —I knew you would be able to do it.

And then the teacher came out ringing the bell for the end of playtime.

*   *   *

Every morning when Roxanne came into the classroom I expected her to take her books out

197

of the desk next to mine and move away to sit by someone else, giving no more explanation for leaving than she had when she'd first arrived. I half wanted her to go: our friendship burdened me, it was too one-sided, I never believed that she had really chosen me for what I was, I felt myself merely tumbled along in the wake of a change that she was arranging in her life. She had been one of the naughty girls and she had made up her mind quite deliberately to become one of the good girls; she saw me as a way of getting in to that. I never believed in those days that she would really make it as a good girl. There was too much of her: no matter how hard she tried she was bound to give herself away in the end, she would overdo it, they would see she was only pretending, that she wasn't the real thing. She concentrated on everything Mrs Hazlehurst said too intently, she put her hands together too fervently at prayers, raised them up too high in front of her face, eyes squeezed shut (mine weren't, that's how I saw her).

I could have ended our friendship any time, I suppose; simply acted so dumb and resistant that Roxanne would have given up and fastened on to someone else. But I didn't. I couldn't help being swept along by the idea of someone changing who she was: I knew I wasn't capable of this, I was just helplessly forever me. And then, I was soon addicted to the heady life of our pretend games. Perhaps it wasn't quite true that anybody would have done to be Roxanne's partner in these. What I learned, playing with her, was that I was suggestible, unusually suggestible. Later in life it turned out that I was a perfect subject for hypnotism: the hypnotist only had to wave his hand pretty much once across in front of my eyes and I was gone. I had never played proper pretend games before Roxanne started me off on it, except mothers and babies, half-heartedly, with my old friends, where the 'baby' hopped heavily along, crouched double, knees bent, holding hands with the 'mother' and saying 'ga-ga', which we knew babies didn't really say. We had only done it because everyone else did. When Roxanne and I played having babies it was very different. We did childbirth first, moaning and writhing against the iron pillars and throwing our heads from side to side, having our brows wiped (mostly I moaned, Roxanne wiped and presided). Then the imaginary babies were wrapped tenderly in our cardigans and carried about in our arms. We gazed into their tiny faces adoringly, we suckled them secretly in the dark corners of the shed, putting them to where we pretended we had breasts, though not lifting our jumpers of course. I don't know how Roxanne knew about childbirth or suckling; certainly I had only had the vaguest idea about either of them. When she came to my house and we played the game there, we did lift our jumpers up, we put my plastic dolls to our nipples on our flat chests. When I fed my own first real child I remembered this, the guilty delicious excitement of it, the sensation of pressing on those hard cold mouths.

My mother didn't like my friendship with Roxanne. She didn't mean to be unkind or prejudiced but she was afraid for me, she felt our mismatch, the inappropriateness of Roxanne's little skimpy gypsy body flashing enthusiastically up and down our familiar wood-panelled staircase, sitting before the hunting-scene place mat at our dining table, pouring from our gravy boat. When Roxanne used our bathroom she would never close the door, she had a funny habit of calling out to me all the time she was using it—'Are you still there? Are you still there?'—so that I had to stay outside and hear her tinkling, scrunching the toilet paper. The smell she left behind her was alien. I knew that every time one of the Aunties turned up after tea to take Roxanne back to the Homes, my mother had to restrain herself from looking round to see if Roxanne had taken anything, which was awful and made us both ashamed. She also felt guilty that Daddy, who didn't like to get the car out, wouldn't give them a lift home, so that they had to wait for the bus. We lived across the Downs, in a street of trees and big detached houses with fake half-timbering, although I didn't know that it was fake then. When Roxanne was gone my mother would come and stand uneasily in the door of my bedroom, looking vaguely at my Wendy house, my dolls' cradle, the sewing basket given to me by my godmother, my set of red-bound classics: *Westward Ho!*, *The Cricket and the Hearth*, *Wuthering Heights*, *Cranford*, *East Lynne*. If I finished one of these classics my father gave me half a crown, so I ploughed through them one after another. If he questioned me about them I hardly knew what had happened in the one I had just finished, but he gave me the half-crown anyway. Probably he had no memory of what had happened in them either, although he claimed that they were all old favourites from his childhood. Roxanne had snatched my books down eagerly when she first came to play, but even she found them too stodgy.

Instead she would sit cross-legged on my bed thinking up games. My younger sister was sometimes allowed to be part of this. I showed Roxanne off to Jean, as if I was showing off a forest wild animal I had tamed, but Jean was sceptical; she never refused to play but she turned her mouth down sullenly and acted as if her body was stiff, her spirit withdrawn from her performance. Roxanne made quite a show out of the difficulty of getting the right story. She sat with her eyes squeezed shut, and sometimes as if that darkness wasn't enough she asked for something to drape over her head: my dressing gown, or the coverlet off the dolls' cradle. Jean and I had to kneel still and quiet as mice on the bedside rug while Roxanne searched for inspiration. When she pulled her coverings away her eyes would be gleaming, full with her idea. It might be cruel governesses, or Mary Queen of Scots, or pirates. There were games we played over and over, and games we only played once. Roxanne was always the men and we were the women, even though she was only the same size as Jean. I was often feverish or fainting or debilitated in some way, I kept in the cabin below (the bed), while Roxanne swaggered on the deck above (the floor), boldly fighting for our lives, her sword dangling at her side or slicing the air. We had to imagine that the cue from our miniature billiards was a sword, we didn't have dressing-up things. Jean and I had to wear our nightdresses for old-fashioned-days clothes.

—Don't you have a dressing-up box? Roxanne was surprised, triumphant. —We have them at the Homes.

*   *   *

201

What happened in our lives when we grew up, Roxanne's and mine, is not at all what I expected in those days. I expected Roxanne to be glamorously and terribly destroyed, and for me to survive safely and dully, achieving all the things my parents expected of me. Then actually it was me who made a mess of growing up, although it's been better recently. I had a breakdown in my first year of university, and for a long time after that I couldn't work, I had to live back at home with my parents. I did get married but that didn't last, although at least I have my kids, who are grown-up now. And the other day I heard of Roxanne, through someone I work with who'd been at school with her, not that junior school but her secondary one. I work in an insurance office, it's not very exciting but I cope with it fairly well. I haven't seen Roxanne since we were about seventeen. Apparently these days she's an administrator in the Child Health Directorate in a big hospital in the north. The person who told me about her said she was 'a real high-flyer'. While he was telling me all this I did wonder whether we could really be talking about the same person; but surely with that name he couldn't have mixed her up with anybody else, he couldn't be mistaken.

I remember very exactly the last time I saw her. Roxanne and I went to different secondary schools. I did get into one of the grammar schools although I didn't get a free place; Roxanne was never even put in for the entrance exam, I don't think any of the children from the Homes were. For a while we saw each other sometimes at weekends; it was during this time, I think, that she invented our religious cult. We used to leave offerings at a particular rock in a little woody copse on the

Downs, and prick our fingers to make marks on it with blood. The offerings only started with pennies and flowers, but by the end—after I had stopped seeing Roxanne—I was offering all kinds of stuff, not only silly amounts of money but quite precious things, my bronze medal from swimming, my dead grandmother's ring. When I went back to the rock the offerings had always gone, and although of course I knew really that someone had simply taken them, I couldn't be absolutely sure, and so I had to leave even more next time. When I heard that Roxanne had become ill, that she was starving herself and only weighed six stone, I couldn't help thinking that this was something the rock had exacted from her. Anorexia was just starting to be talked about a lot. I knew she was taken into hospital, and then came out again, and was supposed to be better.

When I was seventeen I had almost forgotten all about her, or at least I had stopped expecting to bump into her wherever I went. I had a Saturday job in Blue, a jeans shop on Park Street. I couldn't quite believe my luck that I'd got to work with the girls in such a fashionable place. We painted our eyelids and outlined our eyes with kohl, we shook our long hair across our faces, we wore dangly Indian silver earrings; although actually my earrings in those days were still clip-ons, I wasn't allowed to have my ears pierced. My father put on a show of jocular astonishment whenever he met me at home dressed up to go out, claiming he didn't recognise me as his own daughter. The craze at that time was to buy jeans that fitted so tightly you had to do them up by lying on your back on the floor and pulling up the zip with string; I wasn't as pudgy as I had been once but I would rather have died than test myself doing this in front of the others. We went in fear of the full-time girls, who were disdainful, dangerous, enviably skinny. One had a boyfriend who rode a motorbike and came into the shop in his fringed leather jacket. He touched her on the waist, and as they stood murmuring together we saw him nudge his knee between hers, hinting something, reminding her of something; she gave him money from the till. We knew that he sold drugs. All this was darkly intoxicating to us; these girls' lives seemed more truly adult to us than our parents' ever had.

One Saturday in Blue while I was folding a pile of cord trousers Roxanne came in at the shop door: I recognised her instantly although she was very changed. She looked impressive, she had exactly the air of initiated mysterious suffering that we were all aiming for. Her hair was hennaed a startling orange-red, not long but longer than I remembered ever seeing it, curling on her neck. Around her eyes and mouth her face was marked, as if it was bruised or strained; but this didn't make her ugly, it was somehow beautiful. She had grown into the painful expressivity of her features, which had been too much on a child. Her loose white cheesecloth dress was cinched around her tiny waist with a thick belt, pulling the cloth taut across her breasts, which weren't much bigger than when we'd fed our dolls together. Without looking at any of us she pulled a selection of size 8 jeans from the shelves and took them into one of the changing cubicles. I stood around wondering whether to speak to her. I thought she hadn't recognised me, perhaps because she was high on something: her eyes were very wide open and she lifted her feet as if she had to pull them up because the floor was sticky. Or perhaps she had just moved away into such a different life that she had blanked all memory of our friendship from her awareness.

After a long time she came out again from the cubicle, and it was obvious to me at once that she was wearing a couple of the pairs of jeans under her dress. She walked without any special haste straight to the shop door. Probably even if I hadn't known her I wouldn't have dared say anything: I was too shy to undergo the awful exposure of accusing anyone, incurring their contempt. Then as Roxanne walked out of the door she gave me one quick straight look, boldly into my face, and flashed her smile at me, like a flare of light illuminating the whole place, melting me. And I thought: I will always be the tame one, watching while she risks everything.

I believed then that this meant I would be safe, at least.

Post-production

Albert Arno, the film director, dropped dead at his home in the middle of a sentence. It was early evening and his wife Lynne was lifting a dish of potato gratin out of the oven. Albert came out of the downstairs shower room, one striped towel wrapped round his waist, rubbing his neck with another: a fit man in his mid-sixties, not tall, with a thick white torso and a shock of silvering hair.

—Oh good, he said, seeing her lift out the dish in padded oven gloves. —I'm hungry, I . . .

Then he dropped to the floor as dramatically as if he'd been felled by a blow from behind. While she dashed down the gratin dish on the kitchen surface, Lynne thought that was what must have happened, though she couldn't see what had hit him; he hadn't shouted or given out any noise except an abrupt exhalation of surprise, as if the breath was knocked out of him. When his weight hit the floor the noise was awful. A wooden stool went flying with a clatter. Lynne ran over thinking she was going to help him up; when she touched his chest, she knew that it was empty.

Albert was still warm, he was still unmistakably himself, as he had bccn in thc fullness of his energetic towelling a few seconds ago. Lynne couldn't take in that it wasn't possible to re-enter those seconds and pull things back into their real, familiar order. He had fallen awkwardly, on his back but twisted to one side, legs splayed; the towel round his waist had untwisted and she pulled it across to cover his suddenly vulnerable

206

penis, exposed limp in its nest of hair. She couldn't possibly lift him; yet she could feel the cold coming up through these old slates, laid directly on the earth. Even as she snatched at the phone, dialling 999, she was running through into the boiler room behind the kitchen. She could use the old picnic blankets, kept folded on a shelf. The boiler was ticking over comfortably, privately, as if everything were going on as usual.

Albert's eyes were open. That was the worst thing, Lynne thought. There was some shame involved in his blind stare: he was caught out, or she was caught out, seeing him see nothing. Trying to tuck the blankets in around him, she wasn't aware that she was making some kind of hiccuping noise, low-level crying, until she tried to talk at the same time to the emergency services. Then she consciously calmed herself down. She must take charge. They told her the ambulance would be with her within twenty to thirty minutes. The house was at the back of beyond, in rural Dorset.

—I'm going to call my husband's brother, she said. —He knows first aid.

At the idea of calling Ben, Albert's producer and business partner, the squeezing around Lynne's heart eased somewhat. Ben almost lived with them, they saw him every day; Lynne imagined the phone breaking in on the peace of his little cottage, ten minutes' walk away. Now, he would be turning down the classical music he was listening to, or putting down his book. She felt dread and regret at the news she had to pour out for him, curdling everything.

—I'm on my way, he said. —Hold on.

Lynne's son Tom, Albert's stepson, was asleep

in his room upstairs. She had thought Tom would come running when he heard the crash; but the fall—and her cry, she must have cried out—might not have woken him, the house had thick old walls. Tom had been sleeping a lot since he'd been home (he was depressed, he was threatening that he wouldn't go back to finish his degree at Oxford). Lynne couldn't worry about him, at this moment. It was using up all of her work, sitting beside her husband's body, holding on to his unresponsive hand.

—Ben's on his way, she reassured him.

Those minutes, when she had the house all to herself, were mysteriously rich. Whatever was coming had not broken yet, in the adrenalin rush of the moment, over her head. Would it be grief? What would that be like? She stood up once and crossed the kitchen to open the back door, to listen for Ben. Outside, the moon stood in a blurry ring of bronze light. Hail that had fallen earlier was scattered in its tiny perfect spheres on the grass and the paths and the roofs of the outhouses which were workshops and studios, making them luminous. The sculptures—a stone nymph and garlanded boy, a warrior made from scrap metal—seemed alive, caught mid-movement. It was so quiet. Albert had a big voice; if he was talking on the telephone, you couldn't carry on your own conversation, you weren't meant to. Even in his taciturn moods he was always on the move, banging doors, running the bath or the shower, playing loud music or the radio.

Ben arrived in the Lamborghini, tyres crunched on the frozen gravel, the luxuriating engine cut. Then he was with her in the kitchen, kneeling beside Albert, feeling for a pulse. Ben didn't look anything like his brother. Albert's hair had been jet black when she first knew him, his beard grew strongly, his mouth was red and wet; Ben had pale hair, a long, mournful intelligent face. Albert looked like their Jewish mother.

—He's gone, sweetheart, Ben said; and he reached over and closed Albert's eyes.

—Isn't there anything we ought to try?

—No. Leave him in his peace.

Tears were rolling down Ben's cheeks, although he was quite calm; Lynne was surprised at herself, that she wasn't crying. He clasped her against him, she felt waves of weeping shuddering through her brother-in-law's diaphragm. After a minute or two, however, when he put her gently away from him, he didn't look in the least ravaged or out of control. He arranged Albert's body so that he was lying on his back, covered neatly with the blankets. Then he turned off the oven and began cleaning up the mess, with bowls of soapy water: where Lynne had slammed down the potato gratin on the ceramic-tiled kitchen surface, she had cracked the dish, and the creamy fatty juices were trickling down the front of the cupboards and into a pool on the floor. She hadn't even noticed this, all the time she was sitting there alone with Albert.

—You go with him, Ben said when the ambulance came. —I'll take care of Tom. I'll tell him what's happened. I'll drive to the hospital as soon as I've done that. I'll come and get you.

*　　　*　　　*

Lynne assumed that without Albert, the whole film enterprise that had been their lives would grind to

209

a halt for ever. Albert had been the genius, the rest of them had simply gone along with him. When she'd met and married him, eighteen years ago (Tom was just two years old), the machinery of Albert's importance and career had already been in place; she'd never known him when he wasn't a famous man. She had worked on films before she met him, but only in a production office, she wasn't creative. In the days following the funeral Lynne recovered all the old worshipping love she'd felt for Albert when they were first together. Sleep was the worst, because she had to wake up to the loss all over again.

She began to understand that *Elective Affinities* could not be abandoned. The completion guarantee would fund them to bring in another director—only Ros apparently wanted to finish it without outside help. Ros was Albert's indispensable editor, his partner in vision (he had called her that). Diminutive and fiery, she had come to the funeral in dark glasses, face ugly from weeping, her long mass of dyed bright-auburn curls tied back in a black scarf. Ben said she had all Albert's notes, she'd been at his side every moment of filming.

Lynne doubted. —How can we know for sure what was in Albert's mind?

Ben made her understand that they had to go ahead, in any case, whoever took over. Anyway, how could they not finish it? The film was in the can, it was going to be something beautiful.

Later she stood in front of the full-length mirror in the bedroom she had shared with Albert, wearing her long silk ecru nightdress trimmed in chocolate lace—now he was gone, she saw she was too old for it, in her fifties. Her skin was chalky, her cheekbones jutted, her hair was dry as straw. When she heard Ben's key turn in the front door, she called to him to come upstairs. He had been in and out of the house all day, there was always business to transact from the office. Lynne felt self-conscious in her nightdress; Ben was in his camel overcoat, his long cheeks pink from his walk up from the cottage. The bedroom must seem stiflingly hot to anyone coming in from outside. He said he was worried he'd been overbearing when he quashed her doubts about going ahead with the film. —It's your call, you ought to have the last word. It doesn't matter what Ros thinks. Maybe you'd rather we brought in another director? Take time to think about it.

She didn't need time. They must have Ros, to do justice to the film.

She knew Ben, how under his controlled surface his conscience laboured subtly and was always in turmoil. Now that Albert was dead, she had become part of what he had to worry over.

*   *   *

Tom flung himself full length on the bed, face down, voice muffled in the pillows.

—What's Ben sniffing round after?

Lynne was taking off her make-up at the dressing table. —Ben's so loyal, looking out for us.

—There's nothing old Uncle Ben can do for me.

As Albert would have pointed out if he'd been there, Tom was behaving as usual as if the whole disaster had only happened to him. Albert had sometimes held his stepson off with cold disdain, at other times reeled him in, talking to him late into the night: especially once it was clear that Tom was clever. He was good-looking too, with raw unfinished cheekbones, small blue-black eyes set in deep sockets. With his white skin and dark hair he could easily have been taken for Albert's son, although he was languid and tall instead of blocky and stolid.

—Ben's just a businessman, Tom said. —If it wasn't for Dad, he'd be a used-car salesman.

—You're a ghastly snob.

—And he's homophobic.

—Rubbish.

Lynne explained the discussion she'd had with Ben, over Ros's taking over the direction of *Affinities*; Tom had always adored Ros, he had toddled round after her when he was a finicky baby with a cuddle blanket.

—You're not thinking about what Dad's death means for me, he said, —my future as an actor.

—I didn't even know you wanted to be an actor.

—All the doors he could have opened for me. I'm finished now.

Lynne put her hand on Tom's high white forehead. —It's not you that's finished, sweetheart. You're not finished yet.

—And I'm not convinced Ben is so family minded. Unless you're talking really Old Testament. Uncle Ben's on your scent, Ma. He's after you.

—Go to bed, Tom, please, if you can't be sensible. I want to be by myself.

He burst into loud tears.

—I know I'm behaving like a cunt. I just can't bear it that he's gone.

She put her arms around him, lying down on the bed beside him.

212

—I can't bear it either, darling. But we have to.

He went eventually, reluctantly, carrying away one of her pillows.

Tom used to try all sorts of tricks when he was a little boy, to get to stay in Lynne's bed at night and fall asleep with her. When Albert came in later (he always came to bed very late), he would carry the sleeping boy in his pyjamas back to his own room. For a moment this ritual, so tender and intent, was vividly real to Lynne, more substantial and lasting than anything in the present: as if she could hear Albert's step, careful with his burden, on the landing.

*   *   *

The post-production team worked to be faithful to every last detail of what Albert had imagined for *Elective Affinities*. Excitement buoyed them up eerily and sadly. Lynne was glad that all of this unfolded around her in her home. Jacquie visited, his queenly agent, terribly upset and kind. The Italian distributors tried to pull out. Ros's personality emerged with a new definiteness, in Albert's absence: forthright, reckless in her personal relations, with a scalding flaring humour. She quarrelled with the indispensable Leo, Ben's assistant. With Lynne she was guarded, they didn't talk much, though scrupulously she invited Lynne to look at the cut sequences as they came together. Lynne said she'd rather wait and see the whole thing. Two little furrows of misery had settled in the golden skin of Ros's face, beside the brightly red-lipsticked mouth; she often wore her dark glasses, which looked affected in the middle of

213

winter. In February she turned forty. —Don't dare say one word, anyone! she warned one Monday morning, unwinding her scarf from round her head in the kitchen, shaking heavy silver earrings. She had had all her mass of orange curls shorn off over the weekend. Free of its headdress of hair, the queer long handsome face was bleakly naked, spectacular. Tom, who was wearing Albert's old pyjamas, making his breakfast coffee at the stove (his tutor at Oxford had advised him to take a year out), bent ceremoniously and kissed the gingery stubble.

Lynne and Ben often ate alone together, if the team went down to the pub for supper and Tom went with them. Sometimes Ben cooked for her in the cottage. Their relations were easy, as they grieved together. When Lynne went up to London to see the lawyers, Ben took her out to dinner. Lynne pretended to take no notice of the things Tom said about Ben: but the truth was, his insinuations slipped under her skin, shaming her, changing her awareness of how her brother-in-law helped her into her coat, rested his arm across her shoulders, was unfailingly considerate of her feelings and well-being. He was her dear old friend, nothing of the sort had ever come up between them in the past; he might be appalled if he knew what Tom had planted in her thoughts. Nonetheless, Lynne was ambushed by excitements she had thought written off for ever when her hormones changed.

—He's after your money, Ma, Tom said. —He wants total control of the business.

He surely didn't believe any of this.

—You've loved being the wife of an important

artist. The kudos, the creativity, the parties. Don't make a mistake and settle for a mediocrity.

Surprising herself, Lynne slapped her son hard, leaving a pink mark on his cheek.

*   *   *

Leo organised a screening of Ros's cut in their little cinema: an intimate occasion, for the post-production team and a few friends—Jacquie came down, John Hay who was writing the music, Deborah Jones who played Ottilie and had been close to Albert. Tom was sweetly sympathetic when he found Lynne turning out her wardrobe in tears, convinced she had nothing to wear; they chose black crêpe trousers and a green silk Nicole Farhi jacket.

The film began with the married couple in a garden. It was Lynne who had first suggested that Albert should take a look at this novel, which she had studied at university. His screenplay wasn't anything like the story she remembered: to begin with, he had translated it into the present day. But in any case, she could hardly concentrate on what was supposed to be happening between the four characters—all she was conscious of was Albert, present in every shot as if he'd returned from the dead. She could only see back into the camera's eye, and into what lay behind the eye. At one point of heightened emotion between the film lovers, Lynne was so painfully carried outside herself that she twisted round in her seat as if she might try getting out over the back of it. It had been a mistake to accept a seat in the front row, where she couldn't escape without disrupting everyone.

215

Ben restrained her and put his hand on her knee to comfort her. In the few months since he died, Lynne thought, she had already begun smoothing Albert out, making a doll of him. His cold will had often used to grate against her, sometimes he had bored her; it was a relief to be delivered out of his orbit. But now everything was lost: all the scattered effect of a real person, complicated beyond counting.

After the screening they gathered in the house for a party which was a kind of wake. Everyone got drunk very quickly. It was still cool enough in May for a wood fire in the cavernous stone hearth; when they drank to Albert, they threw their glasses to smash in the back of the fireplace. Jacquie wept, and Deborah—who was sensible and funny, beautiful in jeans and baggy jumper. People made speeches about Albert's rare vision of people, tender and penetrating. Lynne circulated round her old friends, she thrust the memory of the film behind her. Everyone said it was a masterpiece. Lynne thought Ros looked strained and ill, but that might just have been her different hair.

When Lynne said goodnight, hours later, the young ones were dancing in a back room. Climbing the stairs, she had to hang on to the banister rail, she was so tired. When she opened the door of her bedroom, she wasn't sure straight away what it was she was seeing, or who it was, on top of her duvet: she had never seen sex before, in real life, from this angle, from outside: legs splayed, feet waving in the air, buttocks pumping in a motion that made her think of insects. It was as if someone was taken ill. Her heart lunged: the exposure was hers, from having witnessed this. She shut the door hastily,

216

hoping they hadn't heard her, sitting down to think about it on the stairs. Then again, she hoped they had heard her. She had drunk quite a lot.

Of course: Albert had been fucking Ros. No wonder Ros was broken-hearted.

But it didn't really matter.

Ben came out into the hall below, not seeing her, folding his scarf neatly round his neck for the walk home. She leaned over the banister, drawing his attention in an exaggerated whisper.

—I can't go in the bedroom, she said, making a game of it.

—What?

Taking off her shoes, she tiptoed down with her finger to her lips. The party was still audible at the other end of the house. She held the lapels of his camel-hair coat, to explain in his ear that Tom and Ros were in her bedroom. Making love, she said.

—You've got to be kidding. Anyway, I thought that Tom liked boys?

—Well, he does. Though he was going at it fairly energetically. I suppose he's got this thing about his dad. About Albert. I expect that's why they're doing it on my bed. Because they both had a thing about Albert.

—D'you want me to go and bawl them out about it?

—Certainly not. How awful would that be? Only I don't know where to lay my head, tonight. Do you think I could come and stay at the cottage?

Ben was holding on to her, puzzling into her face. He wasn't good-looking, not the kind of man she'd ever have gone for when she was younger and could have her pick. But now she felt the glamour in his steady courtesy and calm, his competence.

217

—As long as you know, Ben said.

—Know what?

—That it'll be hard for me. Having you at such close quarters, and not taking advantage.

She laid her cheek against the expensive softness of his coat.

*   *   *

The four of them gathered together on the anniversary of Albert's death, at the bottom of the slump between Christmas and New Year: Lynne and Ben, Tom and Ros. Ros was in the last trimester of her pregnancy, which sat high on her tiny frame like a football. Ben had moved up into the house, Tom and Ros had taken over the cottage. There must have been some delicious gossip. Ros had mostly been away, working on a new project for a director in the US, then promoting *Affinities*; now she had scheduled herself a break for a few months. She was working on a screenplay, hoping to direct a feature of her own.

Ros wanted to go for a walk, but Tom was too lazy, sprawled smoking beside the fire with his socks almost in the ashes, reading through all the sections of the paper. Although he was supposed to have moved down to the cottage, he still spent most of every day in the big house. Lynne came in her striped apron from the kitchen, where she was stuffing a joint of pork for later. Ben was sending emails in the office. Ros stood impatiently in her bright blue coat, its buttons strained across her bump. Her hair had grown, she was dyeing it orange again, she had it wrapped in a vermilion knitted scarf.

218

—You're such a slob. You ought to be disgusted with yourself.

—Aren't I a slob? Tom commiserated complacently, waggling his toes.

Untying her apron, Lynne volunteered. —I'll go with you. I'd like a walk.

Ros had to appear to be grateful: but it was probably the last thing she wanted. The two women were so unlike, bound together in such convoluted circumstances; Lynne guessed that Ros found this unbearable sometimes, though their mutual politeness had never faltered. Lynne had never said a word, to accuse Ros. Beside Ros, she felt herself bleached of colour, old and ordinary; yet she found herself making these clumsy efforts to get closer to the younger woman. They drove to the Iron Age fort a few miles down the road; an unkempt oval mound rearing austerely out of the farmed landscape. It was a few degrees colder up there than at the house—every leaf and blade of grass was outlined in frost crystals, and frozen mud crackled under their walking boots, though the sun was on their backs.

Ros waddled in her top-heavy roll along the path around the fort's perimeter, hands in her pockets, telling bright funny stories about her experiences in the US. Although she was laughing, there was something dogged and bitter in how she threw herself along faster than she needed to, shoulders hunched defensively. They avoided the subject of *Elective Affinities,* which opened in a few weeks. Where the path narrowed and they had to walk in single file, Ros stopped short suddenly in pain, crouching over. She reassured Lynne breathlessly that these were only Braxton-Hicks contractions,

219

she was having them most days, her doctor said they were nothing to worry about, he didn't know why they were so painful.

—What a mess, this whole thing.

Lynne embraced her, awkwardly through the thickness of their winter wrappings, trying to rub where it hurt: Ros grabbed her hand and pushed it into the right place, under the blue coat. The rubbing seemed to help. It was the first time Lynne had touched this pregnancy; these days everyone wanted to put their hands on someone's bump, for luck, or marvelling. In other periods, it had been a thing to keep hidden. Something seemed to convulse in the hard hot mound under her hand.

—I didn't think I'd ever have a grandchild, Lynne said. —So I'm happy.

Ros looked wanly. —I'm glad someone's happy. I suppose I'll get used to it. But you do know Tom and I aren't a real couple? He doesn't really want to sleep with girls. This is only temporary. It was a kind of accident.

Lynne said of course she knew, it didn't matter.

Walking on, Ros spilled over with her fears, deferring to Lynne as an expert. They were still in single file; Lynne, coming behind, had to strain to catch everything she said. She had never heard Ros sound like this before: unsure of herself, and even querulous. She said she was dreading that she would be a bad mother; Lynne reassured her she would muddle along like everyone did. Wasn't it irresponsible to conceive a child outside a stable relationship? Lynne told her about Tom's father, who used to hit her and then blame her for provoking him. The last sloes were withered on the blackthorn bushes. Usually Lynne came to the fort to pick them in the autumn. She and Albert had picked sloes here in the October before he died; they had meant to drink the sloe gin on her birthday in February, but when that time came she naturally hadn't given it a thought. It must be waiting still, in its Kilner jar on the shelf in the boiler room. When she got home, she would look to see if it wasn't spoiled.

—Isn't it strange? Ros said in a tearful excitable voice. —How we're all four still held together here? As if we can't escape from the pattern Albert made out of our lives, connecting us, even now he's gone.

Lynne said blandly that she didn't think about it like that.

She didn't care if people imagined she was only with Ben for convenience; she liked to shield their relationship from prying eyes. When she took him his coffee in the office, she pulled the door shut behind her so that they could be alone together for five minutes; then she might only sit holding his hand. As a lover, he was decorous and shy. They were only beginning to get to know each other.

*   *   *

Lynne cried off from attending the premiere of *Elective Affinities,* though Ben tried to persuade her to go. There were wonderful reviews. Weeks afterwards, when she was staying with her sister in Faversham, she went to see the film by herself one afternoon, telling her sister she was going shopping, paying for a ticket and slipping into the back of the cinema, where there were only five or six other people, most of them solitaries like her. She could hardly connect what she saw now to her experience

221

of the film at the private screening. Every scene then had seemed charged with terrible revelation; she must have been slightly mad, at that point in her mourning. Because the film was really only a comedy, a love story, or a grown-up succession of love stories, tracing the intricate shifts of affection and desire around a set of close friends. Lynne didn't weep once as she watched, she was very calm; although she also felt herself laid open to the film, the scenes washing through and through her, with their beautiful imagery: winter trees, light and dark reflections on water, Deborah's character's green dress flitting past the windows of a house, her aunt's lover watching surreptitiously from inside.

Lynne gave herself up to the dream Albert had brought into being, hardly conscious this time of his controlling presence. When it was finished, she caught a bus back to where her sister lived, outside the town. It was the end of a wet afternoon, the waterproofs of shoppers were slick with wet, they were tired, laden with carrier bags. Lynne felt the power of the film pooled inside her, glimmering and grey, something to live by. Meanwhile she gave herself over to the ordinary dirty traffic, the labouring stop–start of her bus journey, the smells of wet wool and hair and trainers, and the motley collection of passengers, mostly not talking to one another, only into their mobiles.

Acknowledgements

'Married Love', 'Friendly Fire', 'A Mouthful of Cut Glass', 'The Trojan Prince', 'The Godchildren' and 'She's the One' were originally published in the *New Yorker*. 'In the Country' was originally published in *Granta*; 'Because the Night' and 'In the Cave' in the *Guardian*; 'Post-production' in *Ploughshares*; 'Journey Home' in the *New Statesman*; and 'Pretending' in *The Asham Award Short Story Collection*.

Many thanks, for wisdom, advice and stories, to Deborah Triesman, Dan Franklin, Jennifer Barth, Caroline Dawnay, Joy Harris, Tom Nichols, Shelagh Weeks, Simon Relph, and always Eric.